"I'll Pay You To Marry Me..."

Jenny was getting desperate. "Five minutes. That's all I ask. One little wedding. One hundred dollars? Two hundred?"

The stranger edged past her, gave her one last, regretful look and scurried away.

"Do I hear five?" a familiar deep, male voice asked.

Jenny spun around quickly and teetered precariously on her heels. Nick Tarrantelli grabbed her elbow and steadied her. "What are you doing here?" she asked.

"You do know you could be arrested for soliciting?" Nick said casually.

Jenny gasped in outrage. "Soliciting? I don't see how. I'm not asking anyone for money. In fact, I'm offering to pay *them*." Suddenly a tear slid down her cheek. Then another one.

Nick tried to calm her down, to make her stop crying. Nothing seemed to work. Desperate, he heard himself whisper, "*I'll* marry you, Jenny."

Dear Reader,

I know you've all been anxiously awaiting the next book from Mary Lynn Baxter—so wait no more. Here it is, the MAN OF THE MONTH, *Tight-Fittin' Jeans*. Mary Lynn's books are known for their sexy heroes and sizzling sensuality...and this sure has both! Read and enjoy.

Every little girl dreams of marrying a handsome prince, but most women get to kiss a lot of toads before they find him. Read how three handsome princes find their very own princesses in Leanne Banks's delightful new miniseries HOW TO CATCH A PRINCESS. The fun begins this month with *The Five-Minute Bride*.

The other books this month are all so wonderful...you won't want to miss any of them! If you like humor, don't miss Maureen Child's *Have Bride, Need Groom*. For blazing drama, there's Sara Orwig's *A Baby for Mommy*. Susan Crosby's *Wedding Fever* provides a touch of dashing suspense. And Judith McWilliams's *Practice Husband* is warmly emotional.

There is something for everyone here at Desire! I hope you enjoy each and every one of these love stories.

Lucia Macro

Senior Editor

Please address questions and book requests to:
Silhouette Reader Service
U.S.: 3010 Walden Ave., P.O. Box 1325, Buffalo, NY 14269
Canadian: P.O. Box 609, Fort Erie, Ont. L2A 5X3

MAUREEN CHILD
HAVE BRIDE, NEED GROOM

SILHOUETTE *Desire*

Published by Silhouette Books

America's Publisher of Contemporary Romance

SILHOUETTE BOOKS

ISBN 0-373-76059-0

HAVE BRIDE, NEED GROOM

Copyright © 1997 by Maureen Child

Printed in U.S.A.

MAUREEN CHILD

was born and raised in Southern California and is the only person she knows who longs for an occasional change of season. She is delighted to be writing for Silhouette and is especially excited to be a part of the Desire line.

An avid reader, she looks forward to those rare, rainy California days when she can curl up and sink into a good book. Or two. When she isn't busy writing, she and her husband of twenty-five years like to travel, leaving their two grown children in charge of the neurotic golden retriever who is the *real* head of the household. She is also an award-winning historical writer under the names Kathleen Kane and Ann Carberry.

To Susan Mallery,
the once and future goddess,
with my thanks

One

The bride wore polka dots.

Elvis was in sequins.

The bounty hunter wore jeans.

And the groom was in handcuffs.

Jenny Blake gripped the hard plastic handle on her complimentary paper gardenia bouquet a little tighter and stared at her would-be groom. So close, she thought. If that bounty hunter had been only five minutes later, she would have been safely married.

But there was no chance of that now. She shifted her gaze to the man who had introduced himself as Nick Tarantelli, bounty hunter. A tall, lean man with night-black hair and eyes that seemed even darker, he had her bridegroom in a grip that told Jenny he had no intention of letting go any time soon.

Overhead, a set of speakers, hidden behind oversize paintings of The King on black velvet, sent strains of "Hunka-Hunka-burnin' love" into the tiny, air-conditioned chapel. The Reverend Elvis Throckmorton signaled wildly for his wife, Priscilla, to turn off the tape player.

Elvis Presley's voice was cut off mid-verse and the small group of people gathered in the Love Me Tender Wedding Chapel stared at each other.

"Sorry, honey," Jenny's would-be groom finally said. "But I guess the wedding's postponed."

"For how long?" she heard herself ask.

"My guess..." The bounty hunter spoke up as he gripped the groom's elbow. "About five to ten."

"Years?" Jenny said, and stared into the black eyes.

"No," he answered. "Minutes."

She knew sarcasm when she heard it and ordinarily she would have tried for a quick comeback. But at the moment Jenny was much too busy feeling sorry for herself.

It was all her own fault, of course. As usual, she'd left everything for the last minute. If she'd taken care of things months ago, none of this would be happening. But who would have thought it would be so difficult to buy a husband?

"C'mon, T.," the groom wheedled. "At least let me kiss 'er goodbye."

Jenny took an instinctive half step back.

Tarantelli noticed and one black eyebrow lifted slightly. "I don't think the lady's interested, Jimmy."

"Of course I don't want to kiss him," Jenny said shortly. "We only just met."

Reverend Elvis shook his head slowly, clucking his tongue in disapproval.

The bounty hunter straightened, leaned one forearm casually on his prisoner's shoulder and looked at Jenny. "You don't know him?"

Her fingers plucked at the paper petals of her bouquet. Allowing her gaze to sweep quickly over the man she'd almost married, Jenny winced at the bright fuchsia sport coat covering the hot-pink shirt he wore unbuttoned practically to his navel. Five gold chains were caught up in the abundance of curly black hair that covered his chest like an old shag rug. There were three rhinestones missing from the pair of dice etched into his tarnished belt buckle.

Shifting her gaze to the groom's thick, full lips and small green eyes, Jenny barely managed to suppress a shudder.

Know him? If she'd happened on the man in an alley, she would have hurled her purse at him and run screaming in the opposite direction. And she'd just come within minutes of marrying him.

"No," she said finally. "I don't know him."

The bounty hunter tilted his head to one side and looked down at his prisoner. Shaking his head, he said, "Hell, Jimmy. I didn't give you near enough credit. You've even got strangers wanting to marry you now. What is this? Wife number six?''

"Eight," Jimmy corrected, tugging proudly at the lapels of his hideous coat.

"Eight?" Jenny echoed.

"Oh, yeah." Nick Tarantelli glanced at her. "Jimmy's what you might call a professional groom."

"Oh, my."

"The only problem is," he continued, "Jimmy here doesn't believe in divorce, do ya, Jimmy?" Tarantelli jerked the shorter man's coat collar and Jimmy rose up on his toes.

"Divorce," Jimmy protested, his voice strangled, "is the scourge of America. No one stays together anymore. I'm just doin' my part, is all. Tryin' to hold together the moral fabric of society."

Tarantelli laughed.

"He's a bigamist?" Jenny asked, stunned. Were there really that many women desperate to get married wandering around Las Vegas? She'd thought she was the only one.

"Among other things," the bounty hunter said.

Without another word, Tarantelli turned and started for the arched doorway behind him, dragging a protesting Jimmy in his wake.

"That'll be thirty-five dollars, young lady."

Jenny tore her gaze from her retreating groom and glanced at the preacher.

Light flashed off the sequins on Reverend Throckmorton's white jumpsuit as he held his right hand out, palm up.

"But there wasn't a wedding."

"Don't matter to me," he said, lifting his left hand to smooth the side of his slicked-back pompadour. "You're payin' for our time and the use of the chapel."

There was a steely glint in Elvis's eyes that Jenny was sure the real Elvis would never have approved of. Still, she didn't have time to argue. Digging into her tiny, red vinyl purse, she came up with the right amount of money and slapped it into the reverend's outstretched hand.

Before he could finish muttering "Thank ya vera much," she was out the front door, hurrying after Nick Tarantelli and his prisoner.

A bounty hunter, she thought. Who would have guessed that such people really existed? The last time she'd heard the words bounty hunter spoken, she was watching a John Wayne movie.

Shaking his head, Nick opened the car door, helped a handcuffed Jimmy into the front seat, then closed the door, making sure it was locked. He'd already lost Jimmy once that day and he wasn't about to do *that* again.

As he stepped around the back of his nondescript brown sedan, Nick heard the distinctive click of high heels approaching. Grimacing, he glanced at the watch on his left wrist—8:00 p.m. He'd been running all over Vegas since nine that morning looking for

Jimmy "the Lip" Baldini, and he was tired. Too tired to have to listen to a jilted bride.

Especially one too dumb to know how lucky she was.

"Mr.," she said, and Nick groaned. "I'm sorry," she went on. "I can't remember your name."

"Tarantelli," he told her. "Nick Tarantelli."

"Of course."

She stopped right beside him and Nick looked down into her big blue eyes. Pretty, he thought absently. Too damned pretty to have to settle for a husband like Jimmy.

Even as that thought entered his mind, though, Nick backed off. It didn't matter how pretty she was, he told himself. She was none of his concern and that was just the way it was going to stay.

"Lady," he said, his voice gruff, "I'm tired, hungry and cranky." Crossing his arms over his chest, he added, "And in no mood to listen to tales of the lovelorn."

"Then how about listening to reason?"

Nick's eyebrows lifted. She wasn't easily put off, he would give her that. Quickly his sharp gaze swept over her in assessment. About five foot six, he thought, and every inch nicely packed. She had the curves of a Vegas showgirl, even if she didn't seem to have much taste in clothes.

Her red dress with its giant polka dots didn't do much for her, in his opinion, but he did like the way it clung to her impressive breasts. The hem of the dress stopped at midthigh, giving him quite a view of her short but shapely legs. Then he noticed the teeteringly high heels she wore on her feet and mentally adjusted her height accordingly. Without those ridiculous shoes, she was probably no more than five-two, tops.

"Have you seen enough?" she asked.

He slowly lifted his gaze to hers. "For now."

Her lips pursed briefly, then she seemed to gather herself together and a forced smile curved her mouth. "Mr. Tarantelli..." she began.

"Nick."

"Nick." She nodded then folded her hands together tightly at her waist. "If I could just explain."

"Lady, you don't need to explain yourself to me." As a matter of fact, he hoped she wouldn't. He didn't want to know any more than he already did. Determinedly, he stepped around her and slid his key into the driver's side lock. "None of my business why you'd want to marry Jimmy the Lip."

"The Lip?"

A half laugh shot from his throat before he could stop it. "You really *don't* know him, do ya?"

"I've already told you that."

A hot desert wind suddenly whipped up around them, lifting her short skirt high enough to make Nick start counting backward from fifty just to keep himself focused on the job at hand.

"Mr.—I mean, Nick," she corrected quickly. "What I want to explain to you is exactly *why* you have to allow Mr. Lip to marry me before you take him away.''

''What?'' Her ridiculous statement shattered his concentration and he stared at her blankly. He couldn't believe it. Even knowing that Jimmy was a bigamist wasn't enough to throw her off course?

Nick watched the desert breeze lift the chin-length, honey-blond hair off her neck and swirl it around her face. She lifted one hand to push it out of her eyes and he couldn't help noticing how graceful—and fragile—that hand looked.

Deliberately, he ignored the thought.

''Are you nuts, lady?''

''It's Jenny. Jenny Blake.'' She held out her right hand.

He took it instinctively and tried not to notice how his own grip seemed to swallow her much smaller hand. Nick released her quickly and shoved his hand into his pocket.

''Well, Jenny Blake,'' he started, telling himself to keep his eyes safely away from the swell of her breasts and his mind off the fact that his right hand still tingled from her touch. ''Instead of making such a stupid request, you ought to be thanking me for stopping that wedding.''

''You don't understand.''

''No, Jenny Blake,'' he countered, leaning one elbow on the dirty roof of his car, ''*you* don't understand.'' Jerking his head toward the direction of the front seat, he said, ''Ol' Jimmy in there would've married you, stuck around for the wedding night and then been gone by first light, carrying anything of yours that was worth ten cents.''

She flushed and even in the half-light of a Vegas twilight, Nick saw the telltale red creeping up her neck and cheeks. Unbelievable. A woman who actually blushed! And she wanted to marry Jimmy of all people!

''There isn't going to be a wedding night,'' she insisted.

''You're damn right there isn't.''

''Mr. Tarantelli, you don't understand.''

''Right again, honey. I surely don't.'' He straightened, reached for the door handle and opened his car door. ''Even better, I don't *want* to understand.'' Glancing back at her over his shoulder, he added, ''Now, if you don't mind, I'm going to turn Jimmy over to the cops, then take myself home for some sleep.''

''But you can't take him.''

Nick told himself it wasn't any of his business. It wasn't his fault that this crazy woman actually *wanted* to marry a louse like Jimmy. And it most certainly wasn't his fault that the look on her face reminded him of all the desperate kids in every Lassie movie he'd ever seen.

Gritting his teeth, he deliberately looked away from her, climbed into the car and shut the door firmly. The sooner he got home, the better. Rolling down the window, he rested his left forearm on the door top and said quietly, "Goodbye, Jenny Blake."

Then he slipped the gearshift into reverse, half turned to look over his shoulder and started backing up.

"Uh, T...." Jimmy said quietly.

"You shut up," Nick told him. "If you hadn't escaped from me this morning, none of this would be happening."

"But T.—" the other man ventured again.

"Enough, Jimmy." Nick shot a quick look at his prisoner. "God knows, I can't figure out how you keep getting women to marry you, but I am *not* one of your fans. So stick a sock in it for a while, okay?"

Jimmy shrugged but kept quiet.

Nick sighed and finished backing out of the parking slot. Turning around, he slipped the gearshift into drive, looked through the windshield and cursed.

"I tried to tell you." Jimmy laughed, but stopped quickly enough when Nick glared at him.

Slamming the shift into park, Nick threw the car door open wide and stepped out. The fast-idling engine rumbled dangerously, and Nick's temper was boiling at the same rate. Balled fists at his hips, he stared down at the woman sprawled across the hood of his car.

Two

Jenny's fingers curled around the windshield wiper as she held on tight. Her right hand was cupped over the front of the car, her fingers digging into the hood latch. Her back was arched over the hump in the hood and her head shook in time with the hot, vibrating engine beneath her.

She stared up at Nick Tarantelli and swallowed heavily. Even though his image wavered with her shaking head, he looked furious. Well, she told herself, this wasn't how *she'd* planned to spend her evening, either.

"What in the hell do you think you're doing?" he shouted.

"Stopping you."

"Why?"

"I *have* to get married!"

He didn't answer right away and she chewed at her lip nervously. A thoughtful, almost sympathetic expression crept into his brown eyes. A flare of hope burst into life in Jenny's chest. Perhaps everything would be all right after all. Maybe the bounty hunter wasn't completely without a heart. Surely he could see how important this wedding was to her.

Oh, heaven knew Jimmy the Lip wasn't anyone's idea of a wonderful husband. But she was out of time and out of options.

Although, a voice in the back of her mind whispered, *did a marriage to a bigamist count?*

Jenny frowned and pushed the annoying voice aside. A marriage was a marriage. The rules didn't say it had to be a *good* marriage.

Nick Tarantelli reached a decision then and walked back to the driver's side of the car. A moment later the engine stopped and Jenny sighed in relief. She didn't move, though, reluctant to give up the hold she had on his car until the bounty hunter promised not to drive away with her groom.

Then he was back, staring down at her, and Jenny felt her mouth go dry. Strange, she hadn't noticed before just what a lovely shade of brown his eyes were. In the chapel they'd simply looked dark. But here, in the uncertain twilight, they looked more the color of fine brandy.

She shook her head and told herself she was being

fanciful. It was probably nothing more than the weird desert light playing tricks. Besides, what difference did it make what color his eyes were?

"Why didn't you say so?" he asked suddenly.

"Hmm?"

"You should have said something about the baby."

"Baby?"

"Hell, you shouldn't be crawling onto moving cars," he said, and reached out to pull her off the hood. "You could get hurt."

When her feet hit the gravel parking lot, she wobbled uncertainly for a moment. She grabbed his forearms to steady herself, then released him and straightened. He smelled of Old Spice and something else she couldn't quite identify.

Old Spice. She'd always loved that scent but she hadn't thought there were any men left who appreciated the old-fashioned cologne. Most men these days were more into buying French fragrances that battled with and usually overpowered ladies' perfumes.

But the Old Spice seemed to suit Nick Tarantelli. Maybe it was just the brainwashing of those old commercials, but he reminded Jenny of the swashbuckling type of male she'd always associated with that cologne.

Now she *was* being fanciful, she told herself and dismissed her wayward thoughts.

"You probably shouldn't be wearing those high heels, either," Nick told her.

"Why not?" she asked, glancing down at the three-and-a-half-inch heeled sandals she'd bought the week before.

"The baby, of course. Everybody knows pregnant women should wear flats. That way they don't lose their balance."

How ridiculous, Jenny thought. As if footwear had anything at all to do with a pregnant woman's health. Then her brain lurched, stopped and backed up.

Pregnant?

"What baby?" she asked.

"Yours."

"Mine?" Jenny's palm slapped against the open V of her neckline. "I'm not going to have a baby!"

"Of course you are."

"I think I would know if I was pregnant, for heaven's sake."

"Then what was all that stuff about you *have* to get married?"

He loomed over her. Jenny'd never had occasion to use that word before, not even to herself. Yet there was no other way to describe what the tall, angry-looking bounty hunter was doing. But then, she decided, he probably couldn't help looming. He was awfully tall.

She tilted her head back slightly in response, but didn't lower her gaze one fraction. "I said I had to get married. I didn't say it was because of a baby."

"Well, why else?"

"Because of my grandmother."

One second passed, then two, then three. Jenny waited.

Nick threw his hands high in the air in mock surrender. "Forget it, lady, I don't want to know."

"But you have to listen," she said, and followed him as he started for the car door again.

"No, I don't. And don't try crawling back up on the damned car. This time, I might just take off anyway."

Hurrying in those heels was a mistake. Jenny realized it just before her foot caught in a hole and she pitched forward to land on the hot, dirty asphalt. She managed to break her fall with her hands instead of her face, but sharp, stinging pains stabbed at her knees and palms.

"Oh, for..."

She felt rather than saw him move. Then his hands were at her waist and he was lifting her up from the parking lot and setting her on her feet again. He didn't release her immediately and Jenny deliberately ignored the warmth soaking into her body from the press of his fingertips at her waist.

"Are you okay?" he asked.

"I think so." She took a step back from him, glanced down at her knees and groaned. Through the torn, black, diamond-patterned stockings, she saw that her flesh was scraped raw and bloody. Bits of gravel clung to her knees and the palms of her hands looked no better.

Before she knew it a sheen of tears had welled up

in her eyes. She blinked furiously, trying to keep them at bay. Nothing was going right. Absolutely nothing. And it was all her own fault.

Nick sighed and asked, "Where's your car?"

"I don't have one," she answered, rubbing the back of her hand across the tip of her nose.

"Perfect." He paused, then asked, "Where are you staying? I'll get you a cab."

"I don't want a cab. I want to get married." Her knees were beginning to throb and the palms of her hands felt as though she'd taken a cheese grater to them.

"Your groom has other plans," he answered. "What hotel are you in?"

She sniffed, bent over and plucked at her ruined stockings, pulling them away from her battered knees. "Sinbad's."

"Jeez!"

Jenny straightened abruptly. "What is it now?"

"You want to marry Jimmy Baldini and you're staying at Sinbad's?" He shook his head slowly. "Lady, you're asking for trouble." Grabbing her elbow firmly, he dragged her to the rear door on the driver's side, muttering to himself with every step. "I ought to just let you go on back to that dive. Take your chances. None of my business where you stay. Hell, I don't even *know* you!"

Jenny winced as pain stabbed at her knees.

"But then I'd probably see you on the news tonight," he went on, still talking to himself. ""Tourist with scraped knees murdered in her bed at Sinbad's Sin Shop.' Nope. Can't let you do it.'' Nick shrugged. ''Guilt would keep me awake all night and I already told you—I'm tired.''

Yanking at the latch, he pulled the door open and gestured for her to get into the back seat.

''Sinbad's Sin Shop?'' Jenny asked, standing her ground, however wobbly it felt.

''Worst place in Vegas,'' he told her solemnly.

''It looked perfectly respectable to me this morning.''

''Sure it did. Cockroaches come out at night.'' He jerked his head toward the car. ''Just look at ol' Jimmy here.''

''Hey!'' A clearly insulted, disembodied voice floated out to them.

''You shut up,'' Nick snapped.

Jenny looked up at him and watched as the desert wind ruffled his dark hair. In his U.N.L.V. T-shirt, blue jeans and battered cowboy boots, he looked completely at ease.

A sharp stab of envy sliced through her as she realized that she'd never once felt that comfortable in her surroundings.

Maybe, she told herself, she should simply give up on the wedding. At least for tonight. A quick glance at her still-bleeding knees reminded her that things didn't seem to be going her way at the moment.

Still, a small voice in the back of her mind whispered. *Would you be any safer getting into a car with a total stranger?*

Humph! Only half an hour ago, she was going to *marry* a total stranger. And Nick Tarantelli certainly looked more trustworthy than Jimmy the Lip Baldini!

"Well?" he said impatiently. "Are you going to get in? Or would you prefer to ride on the hood?"

"Shouldn't your prisoner be in the back seat?"

"I was here first," Jimmy reminded her hotly.

"Nah," Nick said, ignoring the other man. "He's harmless. Besides, I want him where I can reach out and grab him if he decides to make a run for it."

"I never run," the prisoner snapped.

She held on to the car door tightly. "Where are you taking me?"

A soft glimmer in his eyes told her that he understood her hesitation.

"Don't worry, Jenny Blake," he said, a smile briefly touching his face. "I'm taking you to the best volunteer nurse in Las Vegas."

"A nurse?"

"Are you hungry?" he asked as Jenny slid into the back seat. "She's a helluva cook, too."

After dropping Jenny's erstwhile groom off at the local police station, Nick steered his car back onto the crowded "Strip." In the bumper-to-bumper traffic, they were forced to move slowly, which gave Jenny plenty of time to take in the sights. As twilight deepened into night, the casinos lining the street seemed to leap into life. In daylight they were nothing more than ignominious buildings crouched behind busy sidewalks. But at night their neon souls exploded into the darkness, banishing shadows and lighting up the sky like some electrified rainbow.

Jenny stared openmouthed through the car windows at the throngs of people crowding the sidewalks. As the traffic shifted and moved, she caught her breath several times as pedestrians bailed off the curb without so much as a glance at the oncoming cars. Coin cups clutched in their fingers, their gazes locked on the next casino, they crossed the street, darting between cars and trusting luck to see them safely to the other side.

Shaking her head, Jenny tried to ignore the people and concentrate instead on the incredible casino hotels they passed. From Caesar's Rome to a man-made volcano to a pirate ship complete with firing cannons, Las Vegas was a living, breathing amusement park for grown-ups.

"First time in Vegas?"

Jenny's gaze snapped to him. "How did you know?"

He laughed quietly. "A wild guess."

A few minutes later Nick turned the car off the main road onto a darker, quieter side street. Here the businesses were well lit but without all the garish displays the big casinos boasted.

When he pulled into a driveway, Jenny stared at the huge, two-storied structure in front of them. Designed to look like an old Victorian mansion, the restaurant's parking lot was nearly full. But it wasn't the beauty of the place that caught her attention. It was the simple white sign hanging over the latticework archway leading to the front door. The sign read Tarantelli's Terrace.

She shot Nick a quick look. "Yours?"

He shook his head. "The family's." Then he pulled into a parking slot near the back of the building and helped her out.

Nick took her around to the rear entrance of the restaurant, his hand firmly clutching her elbow. Even with his assistance, Jenny had to pick her way carefully across the pebble-strewn drive. It was the last time, she promised herself, that she would wear three-and-a-half-inch heels to her wedding.

When Nick pulled open the kitchen door, waves of delicious aromas escaped the hot room and wafted around Jenny, teasing her stomach into low rumbles of appreciation. And the moment she stepped inside Tarantelli's Terrace, she identified the mystery scent that seemed to cling to Nick. It was the delicate blend of Italian spices that flavored the air in his family's restaurant.

"Just because it's Italian doesn't mean it has to stink of garlic!" A female voice rose above the clatter of pots and pans.

Beside her, Jenny heard Nick chuckle.

"I am the chef here, madam." The imperious male voice was easy to locate. Jenny found him in seconds.

A tall man with a barrel chest, a truck tire stomach and a high, white chef's hat, was waving a wooden spoon at a much shorter woman.

"But you're using *my* recipes," the woman retorted. Her black hair, liberally streaked with gray, was pulled away from her face into a tight knot at the base of her neck. Her huge brown eyes seemed to take up most of her face and despite her battle stance, the lines etched into her features spoke more of laughter than of temper.

What seemed like dozens of kitchen workers bustled around the two combatants, paying no attention at all to their argument. Jenny jumped out of someone's way and slammed into Nick's broad chest. He lifted his hands to her shoulders to steady her.

"Hey, Ma!" he shouted above the noise. Jenny watched the woman turn away from the chef quickly. A wide, brilliant smile flashed briefly across her features.

"Nicky!"

Jenny slanted a quick look up at him, expecting to see a wince of embarrassment. Instead, all she saw was an answering grin. She blinked at the transformation. With that smile in place, Nick Tarantelli was handsome enough to steal a woman's breath away.

"No garlic," the woman shouted at the chef, then scurried away without giving the tall man a chance to argue further. Hurrying to them, the slightly round woman clapped her hands, then reached up to cup her son's face. "Nicky! I wasn't expecting you tonight."

"Hi, Ma," he whispered, bending to give her a quick kiss on the cheek. "Marianna Tarantelli, this is Jenny Blake and she—"

"Call me Mama," Marianna interrupted with a smile. "Everybody does. What happened?" She broke away from her son and let her gaze sweep over Jenny.

"I fell." Jenny shrugged helplessly.

"Oh." Mama clucked her tongue sympathetically. "How did that happen?" A fierce look crossed her face briefly. "Somebody push you?"

"No." Jenny sighed. "Actually, I was chasing your son."

The older woman spun around and poked Nick in the chest with her forefinger. "What are you doin', making a sweet girl like this chase you?"

"I didn't tell her to chase me." Nick held both hands up in mock surrender. "Besides, how do you know she's a sweet girl?"

"Humph!" Mama sneered at him and turned back to Jenny. Cupping the younger woman's chin in one hand, she said, "I see it in her eyes. You can't see that, Nicky?"

Jenny looked up at him and saw the stubborn frown on his face before she lowered her gaze again.

"So!" Mama commanded, letting go of Jenny's chin only to grab hold of her elbow. "You come with Mama, now, young lady. I got just the thing to take care of you. And you can tell me all about what my son did while I fix your knees, okay?" As she began to drag her away, the older woman called over her shoulder, "Nicky! Go upstairs and get some of your sister's things for Jenny to wear. They look about the same size."

"Oh, that's not necessary," Jenny said quickly.

"Sure it's necessary," Mama argued, patting her hand. "You can't wear a torn-up dress and holey stockings all night."

Jenny only had time for a quick look back over her shoulder. But Nick wasn't standing by the door anymore. He'd already hustled off to follow his mother's instructions. Jenny knew just how he felt. She'd only known Mama Tarantelli a matter of moments, but she couldn't imagine anyone ignoring one of the older woman's commands.

Nick didn't waste time in Gina's room. No matter what his mother said, he wasn't about to go rooting through his younger sister's closet. Besides, from what he'd seen of Jenny Blake's figure, Gina's clothes would be too small up top and too big on the bottom. His mother must be blind, he told himself as he snatched Gina's bathrobe from the hook on the back of her bedroom door.

As he walked down the long hall of the family living quarters toward the stairs that led to the restaurant, Nick wondered if he'd done the right thing, bringing Jenny to his mother. Sure he had, he told himself. His mother had taken care of more strays than Mother Teresa. Besides, he hadn't had a lot of time to come up with an alternate plan.

Nick's boot heels thumped against the worn carpet runner and he clutched the bathrobe tightly in one fist. He couldn't very well have taken her to her room at Sinbad's, could he? Lord, just thinking about her in that short, tight dress, with her wide, innocent eyes, strolling through the parking lot at Sinbad's gave him cold chills.

How in the hell had she managed to find the *one* hotel in the whole city of Vegas that had more human slugs per square inch than anywhere else in the world? Instinct? Nick shuddered. She *had* been about to marry Jimmy, after all.

And what was all that nonsense about having to get married? He stopped short at the top of the stairs and told himself to forget about the odd sense of relief he'd felt when she'd admitted she wasn't pregnant. Why the devil did he care if she was expecting or not? Hell, he didn't even know her!

Grumbling under his breath, he started down the stairs, still clutching the bathrobe. Something told him that he'd be a lot better off if he didn't *get* to know her, either. All he wanted now was to have dinner, go back to his own place, and leave Jenny Blake in his mother's capable hands.

"So you have to be married by when?"

Jenny's breath hissed from between her teeth as

Mama Tarantelli dabbed iodine on the raw flesh of her knees. "Four days," she said finally.

"Hmm." Mama held a cotton ball against the open top of the iodine bottle and tipped it. When she was finished, she reached for Jenny's other knee. Dabbing the dark brown liquid onto the scrapes, she said, "And you say Nicky arrested your young man?"

Jenny's fingers curled around the lip of the bathroom sink she was perched on and she winced as the iodine met her flesh. Of course it wasn't really accurate to say that Jimmy Baldini was her "young man." But Nick certainly had arrested him.

"Yes."

"A nice girl like you shouldn't be marrying men who are getting arrested." Mama shook her head slowly as she straightened and reached for one of Jenny's hands.

"I didn't know he was a bigamist," Jenny said in her own defense. "In fact, I didn't know him at all."

"Then why in hell were you about to marry him?" a male voice asked.

Jenny turned and saw Nick leaning against the doorjamb, his arms crossed over the robe pressed to his broad chest.

"As I was just telling your mother," she started to explain, then jerked her hand instinctively back from a splash of iodine. But Mama was as strong as she looked and didn't release her. "I've run out of time. I have to be married and I only have four days to do it in."

"What's the rush?" he asked even as he told himself silently to butt the hell out.

"If I'm not married in four days—" Jenny's gaze met his and he saw the shimmer of tears clouding her deep blue eyes "—my grandmother will die."

Three

Why wasn't he surprised? Nick wondered. Looking down into those deep blue eyes of hers, he could see that she believed every word of what she was saying. And a quick glance at his mother told him that Jenny had convinced her, as well. But then, his mother also believed in the evil eye and that she could shorten storms by smacking two sticks together.

Oh, he could see that Jenny and his mother were going to get on famously.

Somehow he knew he'd regret asking, but he heard himself ask anyway. "What does your being married have to do with your grandmother staying alive or not?"

"It's a family curse," Jenny said solemnly.

Mama nodded and held up her right hand, two middle fingers and her thumb folded into the palm. Already, Marianna Tarantelli was warding off the evil eye.

Nick sighed. A curse. Naturally, he thought. On the other hand, why shouldn't he believe in curses? Look at how his own day had gone so far.

"My grandmother is my only family. I have to protect her," Jenny said quietly.

He frowned, unfolded his arms and tossed the bathrobe he still held to Jenny. "Okay, forget the curse for a minute. Would you mind telling me how you ended up with Jimmy the Lip?"

Even Mama looked interested in that.

Jenny shrugged and draped the robe across her lap, being careful to keep it from touching the fresh iodine on her knees. "I spoke to the manager at my hotel and explained my situation. He gave me several names to call and Mr. Lip was the first man to agree."

Nick stared at her in disbelief. If Jimmy the Lip was on the manager's prospective groom list, he shuddered to think who else she might have hooked up with. Jimmy was pretty much a lousy human being, but at least he wasn't dangerous. Jenny was damned lucky it had been him who'd agreed to marry her.

She turned her gaze up to his, and Nick felt a sudden blow to his middle, as though someone had thrown a punch designed to knock the wind out of him. She must have been crying while he was upstairs, he thought. Her big blue eyes were red streaked and there were small black mascara trails on her cheeks. Lord, was he glad he'd missed her crying jag. There was absolutely nothing in the world that made him feel as helpless as seeing a woman cry. Cliché, perhaps. But true.

His gaze moved over her quickly. Her hair was tangled and windblown, the hem of her dress was torn and her hands and knees were splotched with iodine. And still, she was far too pretty for Nick's peace of mind. Obviously the other "husband candidates" she'd spoken with hadn't seen her in person. Nick couldn't imagine any man turning down a marriage proposal from Jenny Blake.

Except, of course, himself.

One failed marriage was more than enough for Nick Tarantelli.

"Don't you worry," Mama said as she twisted the lid on the iodine bottle and stashed it inside the medicine cabinet. Patting Jenny's shoulder, the older woman went on firmly, "My Nicky will take care of this."

"What?" He pushed away from the door frame and stared at his mother. The glare he gave her had been known to freeze fugitives in their tracks. His mother, however, planted her feet and glared right back at him.

"You heard me," she said. "It's your fault that Jenny isn't married. Now you have to fix it."

"My fault? She ought to *thank* me for stopping that

wedding!'' This whole situation was nuts, he told himself. Things had started out bad enough, but they seemed to be on a downhill slide and picking up speed.

"Thank you?'' Mama chided. "For what? Getting her grandmother killed?'' One hand flat against her massive bosom, she shook her head. "Is this what being the police is to you, Nicky? Killing old women?''

"What?'' Nick had been in the middle of dramatic scenes like this his whole life. And he'd learned early on that the only way to fight fire was with fire. "First off, Ma,'' he noted, "I'm not on the force anymore, and you know it.''

She waved one hand at him, dismissing irrelevant facts.

"Second, if I was going to kill off older women—'' he straightened, forcing his mother to tilt her head far back on her neck to see him "—I *wouldn't* start with a stranger!''

Mama glared at him.

"Excuse me...'' Jenny tried to speak up, but the other two people in the bathroom ignored her.

"Thank God, your father—heaven rest him—'' Mama muttered, crossing herself quickly, "isn't here to listen to you!''

"Pop would be saying the same thing.''

"Pardon me...'' Jenny tried again, with the same results.

"That my own son would turn his back on a

woman who comes to him for help." Mama shook her head slowly, clearly disgusted.

Nick felt that hill he was sliding down steepen considerably.

"She didn't come to me for help, Ma," he said. "I *arrested* her bridegroom!"

"If you'll both let me talk..." Jenny's voice was drowned out by Mama's quick retort.

"And this you're *proud* of?"

"Damn right," her son snapped.

"Please!" Jenny shouted, and both people turned to stare at her. While she had their attention, she spoke quickly. "Mrs.—" She broke off and corrected quickly. "Mama. This isn't your son's problem."

"Exactly." Nick threw his hands wide and let them fall to his sides.

Mama sent him one long, withering look before patting Jenny again. "Of course, it is. Nicky will find you a husband."

"Now wait a minute, Ma."

"There isn't time."

"Four days," Mama reminded her with a smile. "That's plenty of time for Nicky. He knows lots of nice boys, don't you?"

Nice boys. Nick groaned silently. He wondered how his former fellow officers at the police department would feel about being called "nice boys," and then dismissed the thought. His mother was way off base on this one. "Most of my friends are already married, Ma," he said quickly in a last-ditch hope to end the discussion. "And the ones that aren't, don't *want* to be."

"Nonsense!" Mama waved one hand at him again. "All men want to get married. As soon as we tell them so."

"Ma..."

He felt it. Nick felt control of the situation slipping further and further from his grasp and he was helpless to do anything about it. He looked down into Mama Tarantelli's big brown eyes and knew that he would lose this battle. As he'd lost every argument he'd ever had with her.

Hell, he couldn't remember a single time when his late father, his brothers and sister or he had come out on top of Mama in a fight. Even those few times when someone had backed her into a corner, Mama had always triumphed. Maybe it was because she was so tenacious. He'd never known her to give in or give up.

For one brief moment Nick wished that the others were there. If Gina and his brothers, Tony and Dino, were around that minute, they would at least have Mama outnumbered.

But Gina was in New York visiting family, Dino was at the casino where he worked squiring celebrities around town. Nick frowned slightly. And no one knew where Tony was.

"I can do this myself, Mama." Jenny's voice interrupted his thoughts.

Despite his own unwillingness to get any more involved, Nick couldn't stop himself from saying, "Oh, sure you can. You've done a helluva job so far."

Jenny turned a hurt look on him and Nick clamped his mouth shut. It wasn't *her* fault that he was going to war with his mother. Well, actually it was, he corrected mentally. But it didn't matter. The Tarantelli family went to war more often than any Medieval Crusaders ever had. And, Nick thought wryly, the Tarantelli's were better at it, too.

Slipping off the edge of the bathroom sink, Jenny stood up straight to face him. But in her bare feet, she didn't make much of an impression. The top of her head barely reached the middle of his chest.

Still, he had to give her credit. She pulled her shoulders back and stared up at him evenly. "I'll remind you, Mr. Tarantelli, that if not for you, I would already be married."

An unreasonable flicker of relief trickled through him and Nick refused to admit to it. What the hell difference did it make to him if she got married or not? None, he told himself. Absolutely none at all. Although, he thought as he stared into her eyes and watched flecks of green shimmer in their clear blue depths, looking into her eyes could get to be a habit.

A habit he didn't want, Nick thought with hardened determination.

When he tore his gaze from hers, he saw Jenny shake herself as if she were coming out of a trance. He knew just how she felt.

"I—" Jenny started, stopped, then spoke again.

"Thank you both for everything, but I'd like to go back to my hotel now."

Mama clucked her tongue and took Jenny's arm firmly in her grasp. "No such thing. You're staying here."

"Oh, I couldn't," Jenny said, and futilely tried to pull free.

Nick didn't say a word. He'd been expecting this. And more than that, he agreed with it. He wasn't about to take a woman like Jenny back to Sinbad's, of all places.

"Sure you can," Mama went on as she headed for the stairs, pulling Jenny along behind her. "You'll stay in my son Tony's room."

"I can't put your son out of his bed," Jenny protested, and threw a wild glance at Nick, looking for help.

He ignored her silent plea and went to his mother's side. The older woman had stopped short at the foot of the stairs and she was staring into nothingness. But Nick knew what memory she was looking at. He knew because he saw it himself, often. He knew because the pain his mother was experiencing at that moment was all his fault.

Instinctively, he went up to the older woman, draped one arm around her shoulders and gave her a quick squeeze before bending to drop a kiss on top of her head. Then he glanced at Jenny. "Tony's not here. You can stay in his room as long as you like. Isn't that right, Ma?"

"Yes." Mama sniffed, straightened her shoulders and reached up to pat Nick's hand before she nodded. "Yes, that's right."

"But it's not necessary..." Jenny tried again. "I can do this myself, Mama."

"No need for that. My Nicky is happy to help." His mother turned and fixed him with a look he hadn't seen since he was ten years old and had smashed the restaurant window with a home run. Amazing, he thought, that it still had such power over him. His mother paused for a long moment before asking much too sweetly, "Aren't you, Nicky?"

Warm, fed and freshly showered, the pain in her knees faded to no more than an unpleasant reminder of a shattered plan. Jenny curled up in a worn armchair by the window. Staring out at the night, she tried to tell herself that everything would be all right. That things had a way of working out.

But her mind wasn't listening.

Over and over again, her brain counted down the days. Four, three, two, one. She *had* to find a husband. A mental image of her grandmother's smiling face only strengthened her determination. Jenny wouldn't risk losing the only family she had left.

Letting her head fall against the back of the chair, Jenny's gaze focused on a single bright star. If only she had taken care of this sooner. If only she had more time.

More time? her mind shouted. *In four days, you'll*

be twenty-seven. How much more time is required, for heaven's sake?

Even if she didn't count the years before she turned twenty, that still left seven long years in which she should have found a husband.

And she could have, if she hadn't been waiting for the lightning.

Jenny groaned, lifted her head and frowned. That's where she'd made her mistake. She'd really believed her grandmother's tales of true love and soul mates. How many times, Jenny wondered, had her grandmother told her about the lightning bolt? About how the women in her family, when first kissed by their true soul mate, would feel an arc of lightning shoot down their spines and into their hearts.

And how many men had Jenny kissed hopefully, waiting for that bolt to strike?

All right, she admitted silently. Not all that many.

But still, if she hadn't been waiting for her grandmother's tall tale to come true, who knew? She might already have a family and her grandmother's life wouldn't be in danger.

A knock at the door shattered her thoughts and Jenny turned. "Yes?"

"It's me, Nick."

Jenny ignored the tiny ripple of awareness that sent goose bumps racing along her flesh. Muttering under her breath about stress and a lack of sleep, she rose, crossed the room and opened the door.

He looked taller, somehow, backlit by the overhead lamp in the hallway.

"I went to Sinbad's and got your suitcase."

"Oh!" She stepped back and allowed him to walk past her. "Thank you." Even though the oversize shirt she'd borrowed from his absent brother Tony was comfortable, Jenny was glad to have her things with her.

Nick plopped the bag onto the bed and the mattress sagged.

"Weighs a ton," he said absently.

She had always overpacked, but Jenny didn't feel the need to confess that fault to him.

"You never did say..." Nick went on, turning to face her. "How the hell did you pick a place like Sinbad's? Stick a pin in a city map?"

Jenny sensed his gaze move over her and suddenly felt as though the old shirt she wore was transparent. Glancing quickly around the room, she spied an afghan at the foot of the bed. Hurrying past Nick, she snatched it up and swung it over her shoulders like a shawl. Feeling a bit less at a disadvantage, she answered his question. "It was the nicest hotel without a casino that I saw."

One black eyebrow lifted high on his forehead. "You disapprove of gambling?"

"Not for everyone else," she answered, though she really couldn't understand the fascination other people had for throwing money into a machine that only rarely spit any of it back. "But I never have been very lucky."

He laughed.

At least, Jenny thought it was a laugh. It was so choked and short, it could have been a bark, but why would Nick Tarantelli be barking? "What's so funny?" she asked.

"You." Shaking his head, Nick sat on the edge of the bed and stared at her as though her head were on fire. "You're not lucky at gambling so you don't do it."

"That's right."

"But you're willing to gamble on Jimmy the Lip as a husband?"

"That's different," she protested, though his analogy did make her feel a bit ridiculous. "Besides, I don't have a choice."

"Oh," he nodded slowly. "That's right. The curse."

"Yes."

He pushed one hand through his hair and told himself one more time that this was none of his business. Then he heard himself say. "So you picked Sinbad's because there was no casino."

"Well, that and there seemed to be a lot of women staying there."

His head dropped to his chest and another strangled bark-laugh shot from his throat. When he looked up at her, there was a reluctant smile tugging at his mouth. Naturally, it hadn't occurred to her that the other women staying at Sinbad's were hookers.

"You're amazing, Jenny Blake."

"Thank you, I think."

He stood and walked to the door. He had to get out of there...before she started making sense.

"Nick," she asked, "I had unpacked some of my things at the hotel. Did you—"

He cut her off. "I collected your...*stuff*, and packed it."

In the half-light, she looked as though she was blushing again, but he couldn't be sure. Although, he thought, remembering the filmy lingerie he'd plucked out of the seedy hotel's nightstand, she probably was. And who could blame her?

Hell, those bits and pieces of silk and lace had damn near scorched his fingers. Even the memory was enough to stir his body and make breathing just a bit more difficult.

"I do appreciate your help," she said softly.

Though he knew it was a mistake, he let his gaze sweep over her one more time. Her tousled hair, wide blue eyes and bare, iodine-smeared legs combined to start a groan building in his chest. How in the hell, he wondered, did Jenny manage to make one of Tony's old flannel shirts look sexier than a black teddy from Victoria's Secret?

Run! his brain screamed. *Run fast and far and whatever you do, don't look back!*

Nick knew good advice when he heard it. Without another word, he turned, sprinted for the door and made his escape.

Four

"She went *where?*" Nick leapt back out of the chef's way and ducked his head to avoid a low-hanging copper pot.

"To the chapel," Mama said, and paused in stirring her spaghetti sauce only long enough to thoughtfully tap one finger against her chin. "The Tender Spot?" She shook her head. "Hug Me Something? No, that isn't it."

"Love Me Tender?" Nick asked and knew the answer even before his mother nodded.

"That's the one."

"Why?"

"Why what?" Mama reached for the jar of cinnamon and gave it a shake, layering a fine dust of the rich-smelling spice over the top of her sauce.

Nick pushed away from the cooking island and walked to his mother's side. "Why did she go back to the chapel, damn it?"

Mama gasped, glared up at her oldest son and slapped one hand against her chest. "That you would curse at your own mother!"

"Ma..."

"Don't you 'Ma' me. Jenny went to find a husband and it's all your fault!"

"*My* fault?"

"Who else?" She shook her head, smacked the wooden spoon against the lip of the pan, then set it down on a tile trivet. Turning to Nick, she planted both hands on her hips and leaned toward him. "Three days she's been here and did you bring by *one* of your police friends to marry her?"

"Of course not!"

"There! You admit it!" Mama threw her hands high in the air and shrugged dramatically. "You don't help her, she has to help herself."

Nick watched his mother bustle off, muttering fiercely in a combination of Italian and English as she threaded her way through the crowded kitchen. He told himself it was a good thing he'd never bothered to learn to speak Italian. He was better off not knowing exactly what she was saying.

Bus people, cooks and waiters streamed through the room in an odd sort of orchestrated dance. Bobbing and weaving around each other in a silent symphony of movement, none of them paid the slightest attention to their employer and her son. After all, it was just another Tarantelli war. They were used to them.

One of the waitresses bumped into Nick and when he looked at her, she gave him a long, slow wink and a smile with more heat than warmth.

Even a week ago he might have smiled back and taken her up on her obvious offer. Today, though, he looked down into her brown eyes and found himself thinking about a pair of wide, innocent blue ones instead.

It wasn't the first time, either. Over the last three days he'd spent more hours at the family restaurant than he had in the last three weeks. He told himself that Jenny Blake had nothing to do with it. His brain argued that it was perfectly natural to want to check up on his mother more often. The restaurant was a family concern, and it wouldn't do him any harm to take a greater interest in it.

But his body knew a lie when it heard one.

All Jenny had to do was walk into the room and every nerve ending he possessed went on full alert. Nick found himself getting hard and tight more often than when he'd been thirteen years old and in love with his biology teacher.

And the hell of it was, he knew Jenny felt it, too. She had a way of staring at him that set off alarms in every corner of his brain. That alone should have been enough to convince him to keep his distance. But it hadn't.

The waitress bumped into him again and this time managed to rub her breasts against Nick's upper arm. Frowning, he jerked the woman a nod and set off after his mother.

He finally caught up to her in the main dining room. As she fiddled with the centerpiece on one of the tables, Nick started talking.

"You know, I can't just walk up to one of my friends and say, 'So, would you like to marry a stranger today?'"

"Humph! Would it be so hard to be married to Jenny?"

Maybe not, he told himself. But married to Jenny would still be *married*. "That's not the point, Ma."

She waved one hand at him and moved on to the next table, where she straightened already-perfect place settings and flicked at an imaginary piece of dust. "Jenny only has one more day to save her grandmother."

"That's ridiculous!"

Mama crossed herself, reached for a saltshaker, spilled some into her palm and tossed it over her left shoulder.

"A curse is serious business, Nicky. You shouldn't laugh."

"Who's laughing?" Screaming, maybe. But not laughing.

"Humph! You're going to let a sweet old lady you don't even know, die."

"Ma..."

"What's next for you, Nicky, huh?" Mama shook her graying head slowly, sadly. "You gonna push me in front of a truck? Maybe blow up a convalescent home?"

Nick sighed and his head dropped to his chest. "Quit the dramatics, Ma. I'll think of something."

"You!" Mama snorted. "You had your chance. I told Jenny if she doesn't find a husband today, I'll have Dino marry her."

"Dino!"

"There's something wrong with your brother?"

Nothing that a few months of celibacy wouldn't cure, he thought. But he could hardly tell his mother that one of her sons had been forced to buy a new bed because all the notches carved into the old one had weakened it.

"Dino doesn't want to get married any more than *I* do."

"He's a good boy." Mama folded her arms across her chest. "*He* would help a nice girl like Jenny."

Oh, he'd help her all right. Help her right into his bed. Not that Nick himself was a saint. But even he had to admit that his younger brother had a way with women that made Don Juan look like a dateless geek. Whether it was Dino's big green eyes, his understanding smile or the patient, quiet way he had of talking, women flocked to him. Always had. Always would.

It was a simple fact of life.

Like arguing with Mama.

He changed the subject. "How long has she been gone?"

"Who, Jenny?"

"Of course Jenny."

Mama's lips curved in a sly smile. "About an hour. She said she would find *someone* to marry her. And you know, Nicky? I think she will."

"Damn it!" Nick stormed past his mother and hurried through the restaurant. He hit the front door at a dead run and sprinted across the parking lot toward his car.

Perhaps she should have waited until the relative cool of the evening, Jenny thought. She sighed and reached up to push her sweat-dampened hair away from her face.

Late August sunshine poured down on her like molten lava, making breathing difficult and sapping the last of her energy. She felt beads of perspiration roll down her back and pool at the waistband of her tightly belted dress. Her head was pounding, the curl had completely drooped out of her hair and her feet felt as though knives were being driven into the soles.

Glancing down at her periwinkle blue shoes, Jenny told herself that perhaps three-inch heels were too high for weddings, too. Grimacing slightly, she ran one hand down the short skirt of her sky blue and white striped dress, then hitched the narrow strap of her tiny white purse higher on her shoulder.

A blast of furnace-hot wind rushed down the street,

lifting her hemline dangerously high and pelting her face and neck with sand and pebbles. Jenny's eyes closed and her mouth snapped shut, but not before the grit of the Nevada desert caught in her teeth.

She wanted to get out of the sun. She wanted to go back to her borrowed room above the restaurant and sit quietly in the shadowed coolness of air-conditioned luxury. She wanted to get away from the leering faces of the men she'd spoken to. She wanted to retreat from the warning glares of two women dressed in skin-tight, thigh-high leather skirts and bikini tops who were convinced she was moving in on their territory.

But she couldn't.

Deliberately, Jenny straightened, lifted her chin and gave her damp, straight hair a playful toss. With her fingertips, she fluffed up the limp ruffles lining the deep V-neckline of her dress, then forced herself to smile. She had given up her secretarial job, her apartment, *everything* to come here. She *would* find a husband. She *would* save her grandmother's life.

A sheen of tears burned Jenny's eyes, but she ignored them. Instead she focused her gaze on the man hurrying down the sidewalk toward her. As he came closer, she noted the shine on his wing-tip shoes, the pallor of his thin legs and the slouch of his black socks. A donkey-print T-shirt that read I Lost My A _ _ In Veg-as was tucked into a worn pair of khaki-colored shorts. His nose was sunburned, his reddish blond hair was slicked down and his eyes were hidden behind an expensive-looking pair of sunglasses.

She nodded to herself. He should be safe enough. She'd read somewhere that most serial killers tried to dress as colorlessly and unmemorably as possible.

That certainly left *this* man in the clear.

"Excuse me," she said, stepping in front of him.

"Well, hel-looo." He tipped his sunglasses down just far enough for Jenny to see his eyes. Pale, watery blue.

"I was hoping you might help me."

He planted his feet in a wide stance, stuck out his narrow chest and grinned knowingly at her. "Help you what?"

His gaze swept over her, quickly, thoroughly, before coming to rest on her breasts. Jenny shifted uncomfortably. She'd been hoping that he would be different from the other men she'd spoken to. She'd hoped that his personality would mirror his appearance. Nerdy.

Despite her disappointment, she plunged ahead. She had no choice. She *had* to find a husband and she couldn't afford to wait for Mama Tarantelli to browbeat her son into helping her.

"I was wondering if you'd mind very much marrying me?"

"Huh?" He took half a step back, but Jenny moved with him.

She waved one hand at the Love Me Tender Wedding Chapel to her right. "We could go inside there," she said. "Five minutes. That's all I ask. One little wedding."

"Are you nuts?" His head snapped from side to side as if looking for her keeper.

"No, just desperate." Jenny took another step closer and reached out to lay one hand on his arm. He jerked back as if her touch had burned him.

"Jeeezzz, lady."

"I'll pay you," she said quickly, sensing she was losing him.

"No way!"

She reached for him again and he leapt away with surprising agility.

"Cut it out."

"A hundred dollars."

"You *are* nuts." He edged past her, gave her breasts one last regretful look, and scurried away.

"*Two* hundred." Jenny shouted after him.

"Do I hear five?" a deep, male voice behind her asked.

She spun around quickly and teetered precariously on her heels. Nick grabbed her elbow and held on until she'd steadied herself. Then he let her go and jammed his hand into the pocket of his jeans.

"What are you doing here?" she asked, and tilted her head back to look at him.

"Ma told me what you were up to and I didn't believe her. Came to see for myself."

Ridiculous, she told herself, this sense of pleasure that rocketed through her just by looking at him. And even more ridiculous was the strange, shimmering sensation hovering around her elbow where his fingers had touched her.

She rubbed at the spot and said, "Well, now you've seen me, so go away."

"Can't do it."

Jenny frowned, folded her arms across her chest and tapped the toe of one shoe against the hot cement sidewalk. "I won't be able to do what I have to do if you're standing here watching me."

"Why not? You haven't had much luck so far."

"How do you know that?"

He jerked his head in the direction her last quarry had escaped. "Him, for one."

"Oh, yes."

"And for another, you're still standing out here. If you'd succeeded, you'd be married by now."

Jenny sighed heavily and let her arms drop to her sides. "Fine. You're right. I haven't had much luck yet, but I will."

Nick leaned back against the metal pole of a No Parking sign and negligently crossed one booted foot over the other. "You *do* know that you could be arrested for soliciting."

Jenny gasped in outrage. "Soliciting? I don't see how. I'm not asking anyone for money. In fact, I'm offering to pay *them*."

"A new twist on an old business, I grant you." He nodded solemnly at her. "But I think the police would still describe it as soliciting."

"Oh, for heaven's sake," she muttered, and her shoulders drooped. Some of the men she'd approached in the past hour had treated her as though she were a streetwalker. But Jenny'd never for a moment considered the police.

What was she supposed to do? Stand idly by and let her grandmother die? Tears welled in her eyes again and she reached up to brush them aside. Sniffling, she stared out at the bustling crowds littering the steaming sidewalks and told herself it should have been easy. She should have been able to find at least one man in that mob of people willing to marry her.

Another tear slid down her cheek and Jenny absently rubbed it away.

Nick watched her smear mascara across her face and the back of her hand. He noted the defeated slump of her shoulders and the way her chin trembled. Another tear slipped from the corner of her eye and he shifted uncomfortably. Raking one hand through his hair, he deliberately let his gaze slide from her face to sweep over the rest of her.

Shaking his head slightly, he told himself that with her too short, full skirt, abundantly luscious bosom and those impossibly high heels, Jenny looked like a 1950s starlet. It was a damned miracle she hadn't been assaulted on the street. She was even luckier that none of the men she'd asked to marry her had taken her up on it.

Jeez! He shuddered just thinking about her and some stranger exchanging vows. Nick dismissed the fact that until three days ago he had been a stranger to her, too. The thought of what might happen to Jenny if she went on with this crazy plan of hers was enough to curdle his blood.

She sniffled and Nick winced. Sneaking a quick look at her features, he immediately wished he hadn't. Her head bent, she held one hand over her eyes as if trying to hide the fact that she was crying. If that was the idea, though, it wasn't working. Black tears streamed down her face and dripped onto the bosom of her dress where they formed dark, spreading splotches on the fabric.

He couldn't stand it. Even his little sister Gina had caught on to Nick's weakness at a young age and had milked it for all it was worth during her teenage years. Just remembering Gina's wailing and moaning raised the hairs on the back of his neck.

But Jenny's tears touched him more deeply than anyone else's ever had. Her sorrow was palpable and all the more moving because it was so silent. She didn't keen or sob. She didn't shudder with the force of her sadness.

She simply stood there, tears coursing down her features as she futilely tried to hide her distress.

Something harsh and painful twisted in Nick's gut and before he realized what he was doing, he had her enfolded in his arms. She pressed her damp face into his chest and he ran his hands up and down her back in tender, slow strokes. He smoothed his hand through her hair and heard himself muttering all sorts of nonsense in an effort to make her stop crying.

Nothing seemed to be working.

Desperate, he heard himself whisper, "I'll marry you, Jenny."

Her breath caught on a hiccup. She sniffed again and tilted her head back to stare up at him. "What did you say?"

He stared down into her big, deep blue, watery eyes and repeated his offer.

"Why?"

Why, indeed? Hell, he didn't have an answer for that one himself. All he knew was that he couldn't stand to watch her cry anymore. And the thought of her marrying a stranger—or worse yet, his brother Dino—was not something he wanted to think about.

And he didn't want to think about why that was, either.

"Look," he said, releasing her before taking a single step backward. "You need a husband by tomorrow. You're sure not going to find one standing on the street accosting tourists. Why not me?" Nick winced. Hell, that sounded pretty weak even to him.

"Hmm." Jenny nodded slowly, thoughtfully. Pushing her hair back from her mascara-streaked face, she warned, "You realize we'll have to stay married throughout my twenty-seventh year? Otherwise it won't count and my grandmother will die anyway."

The curse again. Wisely, he didn't argue with her.

"I understand."

"When the year is up, we can get a divorce," she said as if offering him a cookie for being a good boy.

Divorce.

He'd done that once already. And he'd planned on never repeating it. But, he asked himself, what's one more divorce? Better *he* should marry her and know she's safe than to have to stand by and watch her offer herself to every man she passed on the street. Besides, he thought with an inward grin. This would shut his mother up, too.

But those weren't the only reasons, despite what he wanted to think. Somehow, in the space of a few short days, Jenny Blake had managed to get under his skin. Maybe it was her air of innocence. Maybe it was her single-minded determination to save her grandmother from this curse nonsense. He didn't know. The one thing he *was* sure of, though, was that he couldn't let her continue to wander around Vegas trying to buy a husband.

"Agreed," he said, and was rewarded by the smile she gave him.

"Oh." Jenny shook her head and laid one palm on the open V of flesh at her chest. "I can't *tell* you how relieved I am."

He nodded.

She moved her hand away from the dip of her cleavage and began to fluff up the oversized ruffle that edged the dress's deep neckline then fell across the tops of her breasts.

Nick curled his hands into fists to keep from helping her.

"When I think that grandmother might have *died* if not for your generosity." She inhaled sharply and Nick swallowed a groan. "Why, I don't know how to thank you."

He wanted to tell her to start wearing shirts with long sleeves and high necks. But in the next instant he admitted to himself that that probably wouldn't help. He had a feeling that she could make a muumuu look sexy.

A soft groan slipped from his throat. It was none of his business *how* sexy she looked. He was marrying her to help her out—not because they were madly in love.

He snorted. The facts didn't make a damned bit of difference.

The real question was, how was he going to survive an entire year of looking but not touching?

Five

Jenny dampened another paper towel and scrubbed at the mascara streaking her face. Most of it was coming off, but there were still a few faintly gray shadows on her cheeks.

She sighed, planted both hands on the Formica-topped counter and leaned in close to the bathroom mirror. Under the harsh glow of fluorescent lights, she looked hideous. Her eyes were red and puffy, her face discolored, her hair drooped damply on either side of her face and her nose was sunburned.

The blushing bride.

Good heavens. Even the open V of flesh at her neck and chest was burned pink and turning darker by the minute. She should at least have had the sense to buy a sunscreen. And waterproof mascara.

But then again, Jenny thought as she straightened and finger-combed her hair, how could she be expected to think of everyday trivialities when her grandmother's life was at stake?

A new song began to play and the music boomed from a huge speaker hidden among the pink blooms of a plastic oleander bush in the corner of the ladies' room. "Jailhouse Rock." Jenny grimaced at her reflection. The song hardly seemed appropriate for a wedding chapel.

But then again...she distinctly remembered the look on Nick's face when they walked into the chapel. He'd looked like a man walking his last mile. Perhaps "Jailhouse Rock" was just the right tune.

"Well," she said to her mirrored image, "does he think *I'm* thrilled with the way things have turned out?" A hank of hair fell down over one eye and she pushed it back. "After all, if he hadn't arrested Mr. Lip, I'd already be married and he wouldn't have had to bother at all."

She jerked herself a nod, then frowned when her hair flopped forward again. Making one last attempt, Jenny shoved it back behind her ears, futilely fluffed her ruffled collar and picked up her purse. No sense in staying in the bathroom. She had to get out there sooner or later.

Besides, there was definitely an "up" side to this marriage. As long as she had to be married for a year, she'd rather do it with Nick Tarantelli than Jimmy the Lip Baldini.

Her fingers curled around the cut-glass doorknob and squeezed. An overwhelming and unexpected case of nerves shot through her system, leaving her stomach churning and her legs shaking. Married. She was getting married to a man she'd known three days and hardly spent more than a few hours with.

Her husband-to-be was everything a girl dreamed of, she supposed. Tall, dark, handsome. In fact, just looking at him walk across a room was enough to make her mouth go dry. But he was still a stranger. An unwilling stranger, to boot.

Jenny stared blankly at the violet-bordered wallpaper edging the bathroom door. Could she do this? Could she actually stay married for a solid year to a man she hardly knew? Her gaze softened, blurred, and her grandmother's familiar features rose up before her, reminding Jenny exactly why she was doing all this.

Her decision was that simple. Not only *could* she do it, she would do it happily, knowing that she was keeping her grandmother safe and well.

Plastering a smile on her face, Jenny opened the door and stepped into a gaudy, plastic-flower-filled bower. In the pink and white crepe-paper-draped alcove, a different Elvis song was playing. The "Hawaiian Wedding Song."

Thank God. She certainly didn't want to march up the short aisle with visions of men in prison stripes dragging balls and chains.

"You ready?" A deep voice sounded from just to her right and Jenny turned to look at her groom.

He rolled his eyes as her gaze swept over him. He wore a rented coat two sizes too small for him, a Las Vegas souvenir tie—complete with flashing lights—and a plastic yellow rosebud in his lapel.

"You look—"

"Don't say it," he interrupted. "I've been avoiding all of the mirrors they've got hanging in this place because I don't want to know what I look like."

Jenny nodded and reached up impulsively to straighten the knot on his tie.

"Thanks," he said, stretching his neck as if against the stranglehold of a noose. "The damn thing weighs a ton. Must be the batteries."

Another smile flickered across her features. Maybe it would be all right. He was obviously willing to play the part of a groom. Maybe he would be just as willing to compromise as a husband.

"This is very nice of you," Jenny said.

"Uh-huh."

"I probably could have found a husband, you know. It's still not too late for you to change your mind." Even as she said it, a small voice inside her shouted for her to shut up. If he backed out now, she would be up a creek again without a boat—let alone a paddle.

Nick looked down at her and Jenny's heartbeat staggered slightly. It really wasn't at all fair of him to be so good-looking.

He frowned thoughtfully and took her elbow in a firm but gentle grip. Slowly, he began to walk her toward the closed double doors that led to the inner sanctum of the chapel. "I'm not going to change my mind and then sit outside, watching you waylay innocent tourists until some nut takes you up on your offer."

"I didn't 'waylay' anyone."

"What about the guy in the donkey shirt?" His eyebrows lifted as he gave her a quick look.

She remembered the last man she'd asked to marry her. Okay. Maybe she had waylaid a few men. But it was for a good cause.

Nick inhaled sharply and came to a sudden stop. Jenny teetered precariously for a moment, then steadied herself.

"Why do you wear those things, anyway?" he demanded, glancing down at her high heels. "Hell, your knees are still scabby from the last fall you took."

"Not true. I heal very quickly."

"Fortunate."

Jenny pulled herself up to her full less-than-imposing height and said, "Besides, that night I was wearing three-and-a-*half*-inch heels. These are only three."

"Oh, well, then. Forget I said anything."

"You don't want to do this, do you?" Jenny asked suddenly, and tried to pull her elbow from his grasp.

"Of course not!"

He raked one hand through his hair and Jenny

watched as those midnight-black waves fell right back into place. He even has good hair, she thought in disgust.

"Then why *exactly* are you marrying me?"

"Lots of reasons," he told her. "Not the least of which is, *not* marrying you would only give me more trouble."

"How?"

"Never mind."

He wasn't about to stand there and admit that he was marrying her to protect her from whatever notion his mother might come up with.

The door to the street swung open and a slice of desert sunlight cut into the cool shadows. Nick glanced over his shoulder at the young couple who stepped inside. Dressed in their best, the two people wore matching grins as they hurried toward Nick and Jenny.

"Is this the line?" the soon-to-be groom asked.

"Ah..." Jenny looked up at him.

"No," Nick said, and stepped aside, tugging Jenny with him. "You can go on in."

"But you were here first," the bride said, and Nick noticed the gleam of excitement and anticipation in her eyes.

"Doesn't matter," he told her. "Go ahead."

"*Thanks,* mister." The younger man draped his right arm over his bride's shoulders and started for the double doors. As they stepped into the chapel itself, the strains of "Love Me Tender" slipped into the alcove.

"They looked so happy," Jenny murmured.

"Yeah, *now*."

"Look," she said, and took a step back from him. "I appreciate what you're doing and all, but if you're planning on spending the next year in this kind of mood, I'd rather find another man to marry me."

Nick looked down at her and wanted to kick himself. Then in the next instant he couldn't figure out why it mattered to him if she was upset or not. He hardly knew her. He was prepared to *marry* her, for God's sake. Wasn't that enough?

Staring down into her tear-reddened blue eyes, he decided that no, it wasn't enough. He didn't have to be such a jerk about this. Hell, it wasn't as if he was doing her that big a favor. He sure as hell wasn't husband-of-the-year material. No doubt, in a couple of months, she would be convinced that curse or no curse, she was willing to do anything to get away from him.

Besides, it wasn't her fault that his hormones went into overdrive every time she drew a breath. Nick could hardly blame *her* for the way he was reacting to her. He closed his eyes briefly to avoid another delectable peek at the valley between her magnificent breasts. His body tightened anyway, just at the thought, and he told himself that he was in for a *long* year.

Still, it would be easier than spending that year thinking about Jenny married to Dino.

He reached up and viciously rubbed one hand across his jaw. "I'm sorry, all right?"

She blinked at his tone.

Softening a bit more, Nick told her, "Maybe it's just this blasted tie. It feels like it's choking me."

"Why are you wearing it?"

"Reverend Elvis's idea." He grimaced. "He rented me the jacket and tie on the theory that all grooms should be dressed formally for their 'big event.'"

For the first time since entering the chapel, Jenny smiled at him. Not a polite simper. A real, thousand-watt, stunner smile. Something flickered to life in Nick's chest but he ignored it.

Until she stepped in close to him, reached up and un-knotted his tie.

The fresh, springlike scent of a flower garden in full bloom drifted up to him and his jaw clenched tight. "What are you doing?" he managed to ask through gritted teeth.

"I'd rather have my groom comfortable than formal."

He sucked in a deep breath and the scent of her slipped inside him. His heart began to pound ferociously in his chest and he didn't know if it was because that knotted nightmare was gone from his neck, or if it was in reaction to Jenny's fingertips rubbing against his throat.

Something told Nick it would be safer not to know.

"Now just take off that jacket," Jenny said, and began to tug at it.

"You don't like it?" he joked, hoping to regain control of the situation *and* himself. "I've always thought that plaid was my color."

Once she'd set his coat and tie on a nearby chair, Jenny slipped her arm through the crook of his. She tilted her head far back and very quietly said, "Thank you. For doing this."

He covered her hand with his own and felt an almost electrical charge shoot up his arm and into his chest. Hard to believe, but even with her face tear-stained and mascara-marked, her hair flat and every ruffle on her dress limp from the heat, she was beautiful.

And he was in big trouble....

"Do you have the ring?" Reverend Elvis asked in a stage whisper.

Nick slapped his palms against the empty pockets of his denim workshirt before remembering that, of course, he didn't have a ring. He hadn't planned on getting married.

"No, I don't."

"That's all right," Jenny told the preacher. "I don't really need one."

"That's the law, honey," the reverend said, then leaned toward Nick and whispered again, "Got a real nice one I can let you have at a discount."

"Fine." Nick scowled at the Elvis impersonator. He was so anxious to have this ceremony over and done with, he didn't even argue with the preacher's ridiculous statement. The only law that required a ring for a wedding was, no doubt, Reverend Elvis's own law. Just one more way to squeeze another dollar or two out of excited couples.

No doubt the old bastard had a drawerful of rings just waiting for forgetful grooms. Sure enough, Elvis wiggled a finger at his wife, sniffling politely in the corner. She hurried across the room, picked up a leather case off one of the pews in the rear and quick-stepped back to the altar.

"What size, hon?" Elvis's wife Priscilla asked.

"Hmm?"

"Ring size. Do you know it? Otherwise, I have a sizer here, somewhere." She lifted the lid on the case.

"Oh. A five."

"Very dainty." The woman pulled out a gold ring with a huge, garish stone. "A nice, faux diamond," she said, nodding. "Just the thing."

"We'll take this one," Nick interrupted the woman's sales pitch and reached past her for a plain, gold-like ring. He only hoped it wouldn't turn green in a day or two. He shot Jenny a quick look and told himself that he would buy her a decent ring later. Somewhere far away from the tacky circus they were trapped in at the moment.

His decision to buy her a different ring had nothing to do with the expression of disappointed resignation on her face. After all, if they were going to be married for a year, the least he could do was give her a ring that wouldn't cause her finger to rot and fall off.

Right?

"Oh." Priscilla sighed her disappointment and glanced up in time to see her husband's frown.

"All right, 'Cilla," he snapped. "Get on back and get ready with the rice."

She shut the case with a snap and hurried off the flower-bedecked altar.

"Slide it on her finger, mister," the reverend said, obviously disgruntled with such a cheapskate groom.

Nick did as he was told and tried to ignore the rush of memories that filled him. Memories of another wedding. In a church. With family and friends. And Angela.

He closed his mind to the past and grimly pushed the narrow gold band onto Jenny's small finger.

She stared down at the ring and couldn't seem to stop looking at it. She'd done it. She was married. Grandmother would be safe now, Jenny told herself. Finally, that worry was over.

"With the power vested in me by the State of Nevada and with the help of The King, I now pronounce you husband and wife."

And a whole new worry was born. Jenny blinked, tore her gaze from her left hand and stared up at her husband.

"Well, kiss her," Reverend Elvis snapped. "I got another weddin' in about ten minutes."

"You don't have to," Jenny whispered.

"This is the part that doesn't bother me at all," Nick assured her as he bent his head to claim a kiss.

The moment his lips touched hers, Jenny felt it. A bright, hot shaft of white light ricocheted inside her. The Blake Family Lightning Bolt. Just like her grandmother had always promised, that arc of electricity shot through her body and straight out her toes.

Her eyes closed, she sighed heavily and leaned into Nick. Reaching up, she wrapped her arms tightly around his neck and held on for dear life. Her lips parted beneath his and when his tongue swept into her mouth, Jenny sighed again and gave herself over to the incredible sensations rocketing within her.

His hold on her strengthened. His arms became like steel bands, pulling her up against him and molding her body to his. Jenny felt his hard flesh pressing into her and she instinctively twisted her hips in his grasp, rubbing her body across his. His hand dropped to her lower back and held her utterly still. A deep, heartfelt groan issued from his throat as he slowly, reluctantly, broke the kiss.

Jenny strained to reach his mouth, unwilling to have that moment end so soon. But Nick was determined. When she wobbled a bit on her heels, he steadied her with a touch at her elbow. Then he released her again quickly and took a step back.

She looked into his eyes and saw that he'd been every bit as shaken by their kiss as she had been. It was as if he, too, had experienced that short, sharp stab of…recognition. Then a shutter seemed to drop over his gaze and she realized that he would never admit to that electrifying feeling.

It didn't matter, though, she told herself. *She* knew. *She* recognized the lightning when it finally struck. Nick Tarantelli was her soul mate. The man she'd been looking for most of her adult life. But how was she going to convince him of that before their year together was up?

"Sixty-five dollars," Reverend Elvis announced, splintering the stunned silence.

Jenny blinked and turned to look at the man in the white-sequined jumpsuit. "It was only thirty-five the other night." She reached for her purse but Nick waved her off.

"Ring's extra," he said. "So's the rice."

"What rice?" Nick asked just before a handful of tiny white grains hit him dead in the face.

Nick swiped one hand across his face then reached into his pocket for his wallet. Glancing up at Priscilla just before she pitched another fistful of rice at him, he said, "Thanks."

"My Nicky, *married!*" Mama lifted one corner of her spotless white apron to dab unnecessarily at dry eyes. "I'm so happy!"

A few of the bus people applauded again, but Nick sent them a glare that shut them all up in a hurry. Turning back to his mother, he said, "Knock it off,

Ma. You know exactly why we got married, so don't make this something it isn't.''

"Married is married,'' Mama told him, and reached for Jenny again. She enveloped the younger woman in an all-consuming hug for several long moments before releasing her to turn on Nick again. "You couldn't invite me to the wedding?"

"I give up." Nick leaned one hip against the cooking island and ignored the chef's icy glare.

"It all happened so fast, Mama,'' Jenny started to explain despite the look Nick sent her.

"No matter, no matter.'' Mama scowled at her oldest son. "I'm only a mother. Not important.''

"Ma…''

"The *important* thing is that Nicky is married. And to such a nice girl, too.'' The older woman spun around to face Jenny. "Are you Italian?''

"No, I'm sorry.''

Mama shrugged and waved both hands in the air as if to wipe away her own question. "You're hungry, right?''

"Well…'' Jenny said hopefully.

"No.'' Nick moved away from the chef, who was fingering the razor-sharp edge of a carving knife, to take Jenny's elbow. "We're not staying for dinner. We only stopped by to pick up Jenny's things.''

"Ahhh…'' Mama nodded sagely.

"Don't start, Ma.''

"I didn't say anything.''

"I know what you're thinking.''

"Oh, so you're a mind reader, too?"

"I think we all should—" Jenny tried to interrupt, but the two other people paid no attention to her.

"I don't need a special talent to know what you're thinking, Ma."

"Good. You stay outside my head, Nicky."

"As long as you don't do anything stupid."

"Nick," Jenny said, determined to be heard. "Why don't we—"

"Stupid?" Mama shouted. "You're calling your own mother stupid?"

"I didn't say that."

"Excuse me!" Jenny shouted. Both of them turned to look at her. "Nick, why don't you come upstairs and help me with my bag? Mama, we'll come see you tomorrow, all right?"

"Well, sure," Mama told her.

"Fine, then. That's settled." Jenny started toward the stairs.

Nick watched her go and couldn't help letting his gaze drop to the swing of her hips and the delectable swish of her short skirt. And her legs, he thought. For a tiny woman, she had great legs.

He felt his mother's sharp-eyed stare and straightened. "See ya tomorrow, Ma."

"Fine, fine," Mama said as she watched her son quickly follow his new wife.

"Madam," the chef said stoically. "You are disrupting my kitchen."

Mama smiled. "Did you see, Sam," she asked,

"how my Nicky watches her?" She tapped one finger against her chin and mumbled, "This Jenny. She's Nicky's chance to be happy. But he's so stubborn, he won't notice until it's too late." Mama shook her index finger at the chef, who wisely backed up. "I'm going to have to help him."

Sam frowned. "I don't think he needs any help."

"Ha!" Mama exclaimed. "He's a man, isn't he?"

Six

Jenny set the loaf of still-steaming French bread on a wire rack to cool, then leaned back against the tile counter. Her gaze swept over the compact kitchen and she allowed herself a small, satisfied smile.

Everything was gleaming. From the top of the refrigerator to the blue and white linoleum. She'd spent the past three days cleaning Nick Tarantelli's tiny house from top to bottom. It was the least she could do, she'd told herself when she'd started. After all, he had done her a favor, it was only right that she do one for him.

Although, she thought with a wry smile, the scales were still definitely tipped to one side. Cleaning a house really couldn't compare with not only marrying a person, but *staying* married for a whole year.

"What's so funny?"

Jenny jumped, startled, then half turned to look at Nick, leaning against the doorjamb. He looked wonderful. His arms were folded across a pale blue T-shirt that seemed to mold itself to his muscled chest, his long legs were hugged by worn denim jeans and his booted feet were crossed at the ankle.

Her stomach fluttered and her mouth went suddenly dry as her heartbeat thundered in her ears.

"Jenny?"

"Hmm?"

"You were smiling," he said patiently. "I asked you what was so funny."

"Oh! Nothing." She pushed away from the countertop and walked to the refrigerator. A blast of cold air would do her some good. "Would you like some sun tea?"

"You don't have to do that, Jenny."

She stopped, her fingers curled around the shining silver handle. "Do what?"

"Wait on me," he said.

"I don't mind."

He inhaled sharply and took the few steps to the counter. He reached for the bread at the same time she said, "That's hot!"

He shook his head and broke off a chunk anyway. Steam rushed up from the fresh bread and he juggled it back and forth between his hands until it cooled enough to eat.

"You don't have to do this, either," he told her as he bit into the crackly crust.

"I like to cook."

"That's not the point," he went on, and sighed a bit at the just-right texture and flavor of the bread. "This isn't a *real* marriage, Jenny. You don't have to be what you think I expect in a wife."

It was as though he'd slapped her. Jenny knew it wasn't a real marriage. But every time she looked at him, she also knew that it *should* be. She felt it deep in her bones that she and Nick Tarantelli had been destined for each other. Why else would he have interrupted her wedding to the wrong man? Why else had she chosen *that* chapel? *That* night? *That* particular groom?

Fate, or destiny, or a guardian angel—whatever one wanted to call it, was watching over them. The Blake Family Lightning Bolt was proof enough of that. Hadn't she been hearing about that flash of magic since she was a child? Hadn't she waited for it? Hoped for it to strike?

Now, was she supposed to ignore it when she'd finally found it?

She was willing to go slowly with Nick. To let him have the time he would need to accept the fact that they belonged together. But she wasn't about to stop her own enjoyment of the situation just because he was unable to admit to the electricity between them.

Besides, how was she supposed to convince him of anything if he didn't even want her making bread?

"This is really good," he said, and reached for the loaf again.

She hid a smile. He might say he didn't want her doing anything domestic, but he obviously wasn't averse to enjoying the results.

"Are you finished for the day?" she asked, for the first time noticing slight shadows beneath his eyes.

"Hmm? Oh, yeah." He nodded and walked to the refrigerator. She stepped aside and he opened the door. Keeping the wide, white barrier between them, he bent, scanned the interior, then grabbed a bottle of water. He straightened again, leaned his forearms on the cool edge of the door and turned the bottle between his palms.

"You look tired," she said, and remembered how he'd tossed and turned all night long.

"Not gettin' much sleep lately."

"I can't imagine why." She shrugged, the soul of innocence, "I think your bed is extremely comfortable."

"I used to," he grumbled, picking at the bottle's label with his thumbnail.

A flash of guilt shot through her until she reminded herself that he wouldn't have been sleeping any better on the couch. Instantly, she recalled their first night in his house and the argument they'd had over sleeping arrangements.

When Nick had stalked out of the bedroom armed with a pillow and blanket and aimed for the couch, she'd stopped him cold.

"If anyone is going to sleep on the sofa," she'd said, "it will be me."

"That's not necessary," he'd flung back.

"I won't get a wink of sleep on that bed, thinking about you on this couch." She had looked at the piece of furniture in question and rightly guessed that it was at least a foot short for Nick's height. "Your legs would be hanging off the end, for pity's sake!"

"I'll be fine."

"I insist."

"Jenny," he'd said in the patient tone an adult usually reserves for a three-year-old. "This is my house and I make the rules."

Well, she couldn't very well let him take that kind of attitude on their very first night together.

"For the next year, this is *our* house. Rules should be a compromise."

He'd muttered something she hadn't quite caught, but she'd thought he'd said his brother's name for some reason.

"What was that?"

"Nothing." Nick had sucked in a gulp of air, crossed his arms over his formidable chest and asked, "What do you suggest?"

"That we share the bed, of course."

"What?"

"For *sleeping,*" she'd added quickly.

He'd nodded, but still gave her a strange look. "It wouldn't work."

"Of course, it would."

"Trust me on this, Jenny."

"Well—" She'd folded her arms under her breasts, trying to match his stubborn stance. She thought she saw a muscle in his jaw twitch, but she couldn't be sure. "It will have to work. Because if you insist on sleeping on that couch, I will sleep on the floor."

"That's ridiculous. There's no reason for us both to be uncomfortable."

"Exactly my point," she had told him and bent to scoop up the pillow and blanket he'd tossed to the coffee table. "We're both grown-ups, Nick. We can share a bed without letting—*things* get out of hand. I trust you."

He'd groaned quietly when she determinedly turned her back on him and walked toward the bedroom quickly. She'd had no intention of letting him sleep away from her. One touch of the lightning was all Jenny had needed to assure her that she and Nick belonged together. Besides, she'd told herself that she'd waited a lifetime for Nick Tarantelli. She wasn't about to let a *couch* stand between them.

Of course, she thought now as she looked at the lines of fatigue etched into his features, she hadn't realized the first few days would be so hard on him. For herself, she found it delightful, cuddling up next to his rigid form during the night. Listening to the steady beat of his heart. Feeling his warmth reach out and wrap itself around her. She was so comfortable sleeping with him it was as if she'd been doing it for years. In fact, it was perfect. Or would be as soon as he decided to surrender to the inevitable and give in to the desire aching in both of them.

"Jenny?"

She blinked and looked at him. "I'm sorry?"

"Where were you?"

Sudden overpowering heat filled her and the tiny kitchen seemed to shrink even further. She looked up into his deep brown eyes and wondered what he would say if she told him exactly what she'd been thinking. Then she thought better of it. For now, it was enough to know that sleeping beside her without touching her wasn't easy for him.

"I guess my mind wandered. What were you saying?"

Nick shrugged. "Just that I was finished working for today. There's nothing more I can do right now anyway."

"Who is it you're trying to catch this time?" She still wasn't exactly sure what it was he did as a bounty hunter. But it certainly took up a lot of his time. When he wasn't out driving around town chasing leads, he spent hours in the closetlike room he called his office.

It was the one place in the house he hadn't wanted her to clean. And the one that needed it most desperately. She'd sneaked a peek or two and had been appalled at the stacks of papers, files, pictures and scraps of paper littering the floor. Her hands had literally itched to get in there and put the room in order, but Nick continued to insist that he knew where everything was and didn't want one thing moved.

His gaze locked on the colorful label adorning the water bottle, he answered her. "Just some deadbeat dad. Hasn't paid child support in years. Ex-wife brought charges in California and he skipped. Police think he's here somewhere trying to make his fortune."

"Gambling?"

He lifted his gaze to her and his lips quirked in a half smile. "That's right. You don't approve, do you?"

"Not as an investment opportunity."

Nick nodded, unscrewed the cap on the water bottle and took a long drink. Jenny watched him tilt his head back and then stared at the muscles working in his tanned, strong neck as he swallowed thirstily. She had to drag her gaze away from his throat when he spoke to her again.

"Ma wants us to come over to the restaurant tonight for dinner."

"All right."

"We don't have to if you'd rather not," he said quickly. Too quickly.

"I think it would be fun."

"Fun?" He shrugged. "I don't know. But it should be... interesting. Gina's home from New York, and my brother Dino will be there, too."

Meeting the family. Good. Jenny only hoped that she would make enough of an impression on them that they would be willing to help her make her marriage all she wanted it to be. Her feelings must have been written all over her face, because Nick spoke up again quickly.

"They know about the real reasons for us getting married," he said. "I figured that the family should know."

"Of course," she agreed, but couldn't help wishing differently.

"Nobody else will, though." He replaced the lid on the bottle of water. "It's too damned confusing to try to explain to everybody." He smiled again. "Not too many people besides my mother believe in curses these days."

Jenny nodded, pleased that none of his friends would know their marriage was one of convenience. The more people who treated them like a real couple, the easier her job would be. Why, by the end of the year, Nick would be convinced that it had *always* been a true marriage. Being a man, he'd probably even think the whole thing had been his idea.

"So I guess we'll have to act like happy newly-weds," he said. "At least when other people are around."

She didn't let him see the smile bubbling inside her.

Nick sighed inwardly. Jenny wasn't much of an actress. If she pressed her lips any tighter together to keep herself from smiling, he would need a crowbar to open her mouth again.

And it was such a luscious mouth, too. His fingers

tightened around the bottle he still held. Instantly his body leapt to life, and he was hard and ready.

As he had been since he'd kissed her in that god-awful chapel. Damn it, just remembering that thunderstruck moment was enough to make his heart pound.

Nothing like that had ever happened to him before. He would have sworn that someone had set fire to him the minute his lips met hers. He'd been engulfed in a blazing heat that grew hotter and stronger with every passing second. And when she'd leaned into him and groaned, it had taken every ounce of his once legendary self-control to keep from flinging her onto the floor and putting on a sexy show for the Reverend Elvis and his wife.

Well, he'd managed to survive his wedding and the nights following, but only just. For some idiotic reason, he'd never considered the fact that his was a one-bedroom house.

In truth, the place had always seemed more than big enough for his needs. Until Jenny moved in. Now, no matter where he went, there was evidence of her presence. The smell of fresh bread. Home-cooked dinners at night. Makeup and hot rollers scattered over his bathroom counter. Her slightly off-key singing in the shower.

Don't even go there, he told himself firmly. He was in bad enough shape without picturing Jenny Blake naked and wet. In his weakened condition there was no telling what he might do. So tired he could hardly stand up straight, he had been in a constant state of aching need for three days. And some incredibly long nights. Hell, he hadn't had a decent night's sleep since the wedding. How was a man supposed to close his eyes with a woman like Jenny curled up against him?

Fantasize, yes. Dream, certainly. But sleep? Ha! Jenny could make a dead man sit up and take notice. And he was a long way from dead. Though if he didn't find some way to deal with his increasing desire for his temporary wife, he might very well *be* dead long before their year-long marriage was up.

Abruptly, he stepped aside, slammed the refrigerator door and headed for the hall before she could see for herself what kind of effect she had on him.

"Where are you going?" she called.

"To take a shower," he shouted, and mentally added, An ice-cold one.

The banquet room at Tarantelli's Terrace was crowded, noisy and decorated with pink and white balloons, fresh flowers and paper hearts.

Mama had outdone herself.

After the first spurt of embarrassment at entering a surprise combination wedding reception/birthday party, Nick and Jenny had settled into the party.

"I'll never remember everyone's name," Jenny confessed to her dance partner.

"Forget everyone else," Dino countered, and lifted one dark eyebrow. "Just concentrate on me."

She pretended to be shocked and asked, "What about my husband?"

"A momentary roadblock," he said with a smile, tightening the hold he had on her waist. Leading her into a turn, he went on, "I'm only sorry Ma didn't call me right away when you needed a husband."

Jenny felt the warmth of Dino's hand at her back but the energizing heat that always accompanied Nick's touch was missing. She looked up into her brother-in-law's green eyes and told herself that the coming year might have been easier if she had married Dino. But she knew in her bones that a marriage to anyone but Nick would have been a mistake.

Turning her head slightly, she looked for her husband in the crowded room and finally spotted him standing in a cluster of five or six other men. Laughing and talking with his friends, he seemed to have forgotten all about her. She watched the easy camaraderie he had with the men and felt a wistful pang echo inside her.

There was no one at the party for her. These were Nick's friends. Nick's family. The only person in the room that she felt a connection with was him. And he appeared to be doing his best to avoid her. Except for posing for a few photos, he had kept his distance since they'd arrived at the restaurant.

Not even his mother had been able to bully him into dancing with his new wife.

Jenny tightened her grip on Dino's shoulder as he swung her recklessly around the dance floor. With every turn he made, though, her gaze shot back to Nick. She saw him greet his sister, when Gina, a tall woman with gentle dark eyes and long, black hair strolled up to him. As Nick casually draped one arm around his sister's waist, Jenny felt only a tiny stab of envy.

Nick tipped his head to one side to listen to Gina, then abruptly straightened and shook his head. Jenny frowned and wished she was close enough to hear what they were saying.

"You'll probably be frowning a lot during the next year," Dino said quietly.

"What?" Reluctantly, Jenny tore her gaze from Nick's features and looked up at his brother.

His full lips curved into a half smile. "So that's how it is, huh?"

"How what is?"

"You love him?"

"I only just met him," Jenny said, and dipped her head. He'd probably think her a complete idiot for falling in love with his brother in a matter of days.

"Uh-huh." Dino's arm tightened around her waist, pulling her closer to him. "You love him."

"Ridiculous, isn't it?"

He shook his head. "Nah. Ridiculous was Nick chasing off every female who came near him since Angela left." He smiled. "Until you."

Jenny stumbled, but Dino was a good dancer and immediately swept her up again. Despite the warning chill snaking down her spine, she heard herself ask, "Who's Angela?"

"Nick's ex-wife." He caught himself and stared at her for a moment or two. "You didn't know, did you?"

"Tell me about her." Her voice spoke the words even though her mind was screaming "No!"

"Not much to tell, really. Nice Italian girl marries oldest son, then leaves him for youngest son and the two of them disappear."

The missing Tony. Good Lord. Jenny glanced across the room and caught Nick scowling at her. He looked away again quickly, but not quickly enough.

No wonder no one wanted to talk about Tony. And no wonder Nick had seemed so antimarriage when she'd met him. His wife had left him for his younger brother. How terrible for him.

"Why did he marry me, then?"

She didn't realize she'd asked her question out loud until Dino answered it.

"Makes you wonder, doesn't it?" Dino flicked a quick look across the room, then looked back at Jenny. "He's watching us. I mean, *you.*"

Before she could turn her head in Nick's direction, Dino executed a fast spin and then deliberately kept her back to his big brother.

"Don't look."

"Why not?"

Dino grinned. "Because I don't remember seeing that particular expression on Nick's face since the night he caught me sneaking out with the cheerleader he had his eye on.''

"You mean, he's mad?''

"Furious, from what I can tell.''

Jenny let go of Dino's hand. The music hadn't stopped yet, but she wanted off the dance floor.

"Oh, no, you don't.'' Dino threaded his fingers through her right hand, tightened his grip on her waist and pulled her even closer against him.

"Dino...''

"C'mon, sister-in-law. Let's see how far we can push him?'' He grinned wickedly. "It'll do Nick good to get his cage rattled some.''

He twirled them out into the center of the dance floor. Soft lights and paper streamers surrounded them. The crowd broke apart as Dino swung her effortlessly in his arms. Jenny's short, full skirt flew out around her legs and the room seemed to rush by her eyes in a whirl of color and blurred faces.

As the song came to an end, Dino gave Jenny one last twirl, then dipped her backward over his slightly bent knee. When the room stopped spinning, Jenny looked up, past Dino's smiling face into her husband's stone-like features.

Seven

Rage.

Nick knew what the emotion racing through him was. He just didn't want to acknowledge it. If he did, then he might have to also acknowledge a few other emotions, as well.

Things like need, want, desire.

He'd managed to keep his distance from Jenny throughout most of the party. Hell, he'd even ignored his mother's not-too-subtle hints about dancing with his new wife. Then Gina had to add her two cents' worth by reminding him that Jenny probably felt more uncomfortable than he did at the party—since she didn't know a soul there.

His kindhearted sister had accomplished what their

mother's badgering had not. Nick was all set to go out and do the right thing by asking Jenny to dance. And that's when he'd seen her.

Plastered so closely to Dino that she could probably feel his brother's belt buckle scraping all the way through to her backbone, Nick's bride was the center of attention. As she was swept skillfully around the dance floor by his younger brother, the hem of Jenny's short dress lifted to thigh level, giving Nick and every other man in the room tantalizing glimpses of her shapely legs.

He wasn't surprised by the fact that every eye was on Jenny. Hell, he'd known he was in trouble the minute he'd seen her in that dress. That soft sea green silk set off the golden color of her skin and the pale blond of her hair. The fragile fabric clung to her breasts and despite the relatively nonrevealing collar, it managed to look like a negligee on her.

He'd actually *expected* the men at the party to admire her. What he hadn't been prepared for was the hot, pulsing jealousy that had engulfed him.

When one of his best friends, Steve Chavez, whistled his appreciation, Nick had to curl his fingers into his palm to keep from decking him. But that rush of anger was nothing compared to the feeling that came over him as Dino lowered Jenny into a seductively slow dip.

By the time the applause had died away, Nick was already in the center of the dance floor staring down into his wife's eyes.

"May I cut in?"

Dino threw him a quick look over his shoulder, then casually straightened, bringing Jenny back to her feet in a smooth, fluid motion. Innocently wide-eyed, he asked. "*You*, Nick? *Dance?*"

Music started up again and Nick took Jenny's hand to pull her to him. "Go play with your friends, Dino."

He heard his brother's quiet laughter, but paid no attention. Instead he looked into Jenny's eyes and concentrated on the feel of her small hand on his shoulder. Swaying gently together, she said, "I love this old song."

Nick frowned slightly, groaned quietly and scanned the room for his mother...the person in charge of the music.

She was easy to spot. There weren't too many short, Italian women with Cheshire cat grins on their faces. She even had the nerve to wink at him.

Mama Tarantelli was many things, but subtle wasn't one of them. "The Second Time Around" slowly came to an end, but before he could even think about stopping, another slow, dreamy song began.

Karen Carpenter's sultry voice whispered into the room as she sang the opening notes to "We've Only Just Begun." Nick shook his head and didn't even notice when the other dancers on the floor stepped back, creating a wide circle around the newlyweds.

Jenny laughed and he realized how good it sounded. How good it felt to be holding her and sharing the frustration over his mother's maneuvers. His hand slipped to the small of her back, just above the rounded curve of her bottom. His gaze moved over her still-smiling features and he wondered why it seemed as though he'd known her forever. Why did it feel so… *right,* holding her close?

Instinctively, he brought her right hand to his shoulder then draped both arms around her. Her hands met at the back of his neck and he felt the fire in her featherlight touch. His left hand moved up and down her back, while his right dipped lower, to pull her tight against him.

She stumbled slightly and he smiled. Those heels of hers. If he had any sense, he would throw out every pair she owned. But then he would have to give up his private fantasies of Jenny in high heels and some of that flimsy, lacy lingerie he'd packed for her what seemed a lifetime ago.

They continued to move together in a slow, tight circle, oblivious to anything but each other. She leaned in closer, brushing her breasts against his chest. His body hardened even further and he pressed her against his groin in a desperate attempt at relief from the aching need of her.

Her breath caught audibly and she twisted her hips slightly beneath his hand. What was left of his control snapped and he bent his head to claim her mouth. She met him eagerly, her lips parting for his tongue. With every damp, heated caress, he fed the fires consuming them.

Everything but Jenny disappeared. He didn't know where he was and he didn't care. All he knew was that he had to kiss her. Hold her. Touch her. He needed her as much as he needed his next breath. He slid one hand up the curve of her waist to her breast. He tore his mouth from hers, lifted her off the floor and buried his face in the sweet curve of her neck.

That's when he heard the applause.

Head thrown back, eyes closed, Jenny arched against Nick and shivered when his lips and tongue touched the line of her throat. Her fingers curled into his shoulders and a soft moan escaped her.

When the applause started, she jerked in his arms as if she'd been shot. Her eyes flew open and she looked out over the crowd, still roaring their approval. Slowly, Nick lowered her, letting her body slide down the front of his until she was standing on her own two feet again. She wobbled a bit, but his hand at her elbow steadied her quickly enough.

A rush of heat that had nothing to do with desire raced through her bloodstream and stained her cheeks a brilliant scarlet. She covered her face with both hands and that action brought on another round of hoots and whistles from the crowd.

Nick wrapped one arm around her shoulders and pulled her against him protectively. She drew on his strength and let her hands fall to her sides. So they'd gotten a little out of control. So they'd kissed each other as if they were alone in a bedroom.

What did it matter if everyone in the room knew

that she wanted him? They were all supposed to think that she and Nick were newlyweds. And that kiss had probably gone a long way toward convincing everyone that their marriage was a real one.

"Kiss 'er again, Nick!" someone shouted.

"Yeah, I missed it and my wife says it was a beaut!"

"Your wife probably wants you to take notes!" another man called out and more laughter rippled through the room.

Jenny concentrated on the feel of Nick's broad chest at her back and the quiet strength and confidence present in the arm he kept around her.

"All right," Mama said, and stepped out of the crowd to join the couple. "That's enough beer for Joe Martini," she said, and directed a mock glare at an older, pot-bellied man.

Jenny smiled, pleased to have everyone's attention shift away from her and Nick, even if only for a moment.

Mama waved her right hand in the air until the crowd settled down. Someone at the back of the room turned off the stereo just as Johnny Mathis began another song.

"A telegram came a few minutes ago," Mama said loudly. Unfolding the yellow slip of paper in her left hand, she held it up to the light and began to read.

" 'Darling Jenny stop Got your wire stop Congratulations and all my love to you and your

Nick stop Coming to meet my new grandson stop Love, Tess'''

Tears rushed into Jenny's eyes and she blinked frantically. Grandma Tess was fine. And thanks to Jenny, she would *remain* fine. Best of all, though, she was coming for a visit.

Nick seemed to know just what that wire meant to her. He squeezed her shoulders gently and handed her a handkerchief when she began to rub at her overflowing eyes with the tips of her fingers.

"No black streaks tonight," he whispered, and Jenny chuckled. She really must remember to buy some waterproof mascara.

"And just guess where Jenny's grandma is?" Mama asked of no one in particular. *"Switzerland!"*

She looked down at the telegram again as if she couldn't quite believe the words had come from so far away, then she folded it neatly. Stepping up to Jenny, Mama handed her the paper then leaned in to kiss the younger woman's cheek.

"The curse is broken," she whispered, and Jenny nodded mutely.

"There's something else, too," Mama announced. "The family, we got the newlyweds a wedding present." She paused. "Well, my Dino. *He* got it. But Gina and me, we told him to do it." She shrugged broadly.

Knowing chuckles lifted from the crowd as Dino stepped into the circle of light to stand beside his mother. He bent over, planted a kiss on top of her head and ducked as Mama waved both hands at him to shoo him away. Then he walked up to Nick and Jenny and handed them a long, sealed envelope.

"What's this?" Nick asked, his gaze wary as he looked from the envelope to his brother and back again.

"It's a honeymoon." Dino grinned, both eyebrows arched high on his forehead.

"Dino…" Nick muttered, and Jenny felt the sudden tension in him.

"It was Ma's idea," Dino shouted for the benefit of the crowd. "Then Gina joined in and…hell." He ducked again as Mama took a swat at him and missed. "Against the two of them, I didn't stand a chance. Happy marriage, you two."

"Open it," someone yelled.

"Come on!" another voice shouted. "What is it?"

Grumbling under his breath, Nick handed Jenny the envelope and she slowly tore it open. She looked inside, gasped, then looked again. Her gaze shot to Dino.

He grinned at her and winked.

"Hey, you two, you gonna tell the rest of us?"

Nick leaned over Jenny's shoulder, glanced into the envelope and straightened again. Clearing his throat, he told the crowd, "It's a room at the Taj. Three days and two nights."

"Not just *any* room," Dino corrected, clearly enjoying himself. "Next weekend, my big brother and his brand-new wife will be staying in the Presidential Suite.'' He gave them a half bow. ''Compliments of yours truly.'' Dino shrugged slightly. ''And of course, my employers.''

A thunderous round of applause rose up like a roar and settled down over Nick and Jenny. Under the cover of noise, Dino leaned in close to her, kissed her on the cheek and whispered, ''Call it a pretend honeymoon for a pretend marriage.''

She pulled her head back to look at him. Her brother-in-law's green eyes were shining and there was a wicked smile on his face. Another ally, she told herself and clutched the envelope tightly. With the combined forces of Jenny and his family working on him, Nick didn't stand a chance.

She glanced up at her husband and noticed that except for a muscle ticking spasmodically in his cheek, his features were carefully blank.

Two hours later Nick practically had to drag Jenny out of the restaurant. With the guests gone and the banquet room wall-to-wall rubble, she was determined to help Mama clean up. Hell, even Gina and Dino had already left.

''Leave it for tomorrow,'' Mama told her, and stifled a yawn behind one hand. ''The bus people will take care of it.''

''I can have most of this set to rights in a half hour or so,'' Jenny insisted.

She could, too, Nick told himself. Though he was in no mood to hang around his mother anymore that night. He took Jenny's forearm and gave her a tug. She ignored him.

"It was your party," Mama shook her head. "Guests of honor don't do the trash."

"Honestly, Mama," Jenny argued and reached out for a crumpled streamer lying across a half-eaten pan of lasagna. "I don't mind at all. It was a lovely party. Let me help clean up to show my appreciation."

Mama beamed at her, then lifted one hand to pat her cheek. "You're a nice girl, Jenny." Her sharp gaze slid to Nick. "Didn't I tell you?"

He nodded stiffly. Yes, she had told him. And he had no doubt she would tell him again. And again.

"You want to thank me? Go home. Go to bed." Mama started for the door. "Good night, you two," she called over her shoulder. "Sleep well."

Nick scowled at his mother's retreating back. Sleep well. As if he'd be getting any sleep at all tonight! As Mama left the room and turned for the staircase, Nick told himself that she was getting a lot more obvious the older she got. She used to be pretty sneaky. Mama had a way of getting what she wanted before you even knew what she was after. But now it seemed that she didn't care for subtleties. A surprise party. The room at the Taj. Hell, the music she'd played all night! No doubt about it, Mama was campaigning for Jenny.

He stole a quick look at his bride. A soft smile danced across her mouth as she turned in a slow circle, admiring what was left of their wedding reception. His heartbeat picked up and it was suddenly hard to breathe.

Jenny didn't need any help from Mama. All by herself, she was tying him up in so many knots, he could hardly think straight.

As he watched, she reached up, trying to grab the string of one of the balloons that still filled the hall. She was several inches short of her goal even with those heels of hers. Unerringly, his gaze shot to her legs. Her hemline sneaked higher and higher up her thighs as she stretched for her prize.

He tore his gaze away, lifted one hand, snatched up three or four ribbons and handed them to her. The helium-filled balloons bumped against each other as Jenny pulled them down to look at them.

"Wasn't this sweet of your family?"

Sweet wasn't the word he would use, but he agreed anyway. "Yeah. It was."

"This was a wonderful party," she said, and looked around at the debris-littered room and smiled, obviously remembering how it had looked earlier. Then she glanced down at the long envelope she still held clutched in one hand. "Imagine. Three whole days in a Presidential Suite!"

He groaned silently at her smile. At that moment he could have cheerfully thumped Dino until he was black and blue. There was no way Nick wanted to spend three days and two nights with Jenny—alone— in some sumptuous suite at the most elegant casino in Vegas.

"Look, Jenny—" he started.

"I've heard about those places," she broke in. "I even saw a report on television once about the luxurious rooms at these big casinos." She grinned excitedly and turned in a quick circle, her fistful of balloons dancing around her head.

Instinctively, he reached out to steady her as she wobbled.

"But I never dreamed that I'd actually get to *stay* in one."

How was he supposed to say no to that kind of enthusiasm? Grimly, he took her elbow and began to lead her to the door. "Come on, Jenny. Let's go."

Once outside, she paused to look up at the desert sky. This far from the garishly lit Strip, the stars were visible. Acres of stars shone down on them and she tilted her head back to admire them all.

"It's so beautiful." Her voice was a hushed, awed whisper, as if she were in church.

He leaned against the hood of his car, crossed his arms over his chest and stared at her. "Beautiful," he echoed, but he wasn't talking about the night sky.

"Do you believe in wishes, Nick?"

"What do you mean?"

She turned her head to look at him. "I mean, wishing on a star. Do you believe a wish made on a star comes true?"

He wanted to. Looking at her now, he knew that he wanted to believe in wishes and happily ever after and love at first sight. But he didn't. Not anymore.

"No."

Disappointment flashed in her eyes briefly before it was replaced by a hopeful gleam.

"That's all right." She looked back up at the sky, closed her eyes and said softly, "I'll believe for you. I'll even make the wish for you."

Her blond hair shimmered in the moonlight and the line of her throat looked long and elegant. She concentrated quietly for a moment or two, then she straightened, turned toward him and gave him a breathtaking smile.

A steel band tightened around his chest. "What did you wish for?"

"I can't tell."

She walked to his side and laid one hand on his forearm. The helium balloons dipped and swayed in the hot wind, then slapped Nick in the head. Looking up into his eyes, she said softly, "Let's go home."

A week later Nick stepped out of his tiny office and walked down the short hall to the living room. Standing in the shadows, he watched Jenny. It was becoming a habit with him, he knew. But somehow, he couldn't keep himself from it.

Since the night of the wedding reception, he'd been like a man possessed. He couldn't rid himself of the memory of that searing kiss. And if he was to be honest about it, he didn't want to.

Just remembering the surge of passion, the hot, stinging rush of desire that had filled him there on the dance floor, had him trembling with the need to feel it all again. He'd never felt that...*alive* before.

Every night since then, he lay beside her in a bed that felt as if it were shrinking daily. His eyes closed and he groaned quietly. Just the night before she'd wiggled and twisted her little bottom against him until he'd had to leap out of bed and go for a long walk. It was either that or wake her up and do all the things he kept thinking about doing to her.

With her.

The worst part was, the walk hadn't helped. Talking to himself didn't help. Hell, even remembering what a nightmare his first marriage had been didn't help.

He shook his head, disgusted with himself, then in the next instant, forgot about everything but his wife. Jenny sat up straighter in his old leather chair, set the book of poetry she'd been reading in her lap and began to stretch. Her movements were fluid, languid, sensual.

Sapphire blue satin clung to her curves and rubbed over her body like a lover's caress. It was a simple nightgown, with clean, straight lines and no extra fancy work or embellishments to distract a man from the woman wearing it.

When she was finished, she curled up again in the chair, tucking her bare feet beneath her and returning her attention to Walt Whitman's poetry. He inhaled sharply and forced himself to turn around and walk back to his office.

He stepped into the tiny room, closed the door quietly behind him then sat down in front of his desk. Glancing at the file lying open on the clutter of strewn papers, Nick told himself he should be concentrating on finding his latest bail jumper. But even an abusive husband wasn't enough to get his mind off Jenny.

She was such a study in contrasts. Innocent blue eyes and a lush, made-to-be-kissed mouth. A woman with a sex kitten's body and a love of poetry. Every move Jenny made was seductive, yet she blushed like a schoolgirl when embarrassed.

He propped both elbows on a sliding stack of papers and cradled his head in his hands. Married almost two weeks, she was completely at home in his house. She'd brought order into chaos and she'd done it all on her own.

He snorted a choked laugh and leaned back in his chair. Jenny didn't think anything of racing over to the restaurant if Mama needed help. She'd already become his neighborhood's favorite baby-sitter and when she'd noticed the older man next door trying, with difficulty, to do his own yard work, she had smoothly taken over that chore, as well.

She had an independent streak almost as wide as his own, yet somehow she didn't seem to mind when people began to count on her. Need her. In fact, she appeared to thrive on it.

But she never asked him for anything. Not help setting the table. Not with the cleaning. She'd even fixed the leak in the bathroom sink on her own.

Hell, if she was driving him *this* crazy here in the house, what would happen when they were on that blasted honeymoon? Away from everyday life, wrapped in luxury, with no one but each other for company?

No doubt about it. He was a dead man.

Nick frowned, pushed one hand through his hair, then reached for the pen he'd tossed onto the desk earlier. He might as well get some work done, he told himself. There would be plenty of time later to lie awake and think.

Eight

The bellman pushed the double doors open with a dramatic flourish then led the way inside. Jenny took two steps across the threshold and stopped dead. Her jaw dropped and she stared in mute wonder at the luxurious suite.

Floor-to-ceiling windows showcased a breathtaking view of Las Vegas and the desert surrounding it. Above the distant mountains, black thunderclouds bunched together, readying their assault on the city. Within hours, the storm would blanket the entire area. But for now, the sky was a blue so deep it hurt to look at it and sunlight poured in through the wide windows.

A horseshoe-shaped, overstuffed sofa faced a stone

and marble fireplace where gas flames danced across artificial logs. Oversize pillows already lay on the plush, russet carpeting in front of the hearth as if inviting romance. The iced bottle of champagne and two matching crystal flutes completed the seductive scene.

Jenny sucked in a breath and let her gaze drift over the rest of the room. Huge, fresh flower arrangements dotted the tops of the antique tables sprinkled about the suite and their perfume sweetened the refrigerated air. Off to one side, a gleaming, brass circular staircase wound its way to a loft, just out of sight. Her mouth went dry as she imagined the bedroom no doubt lying at the top of those stairs.

She hardly heard the bellman as he showed Nick around the suite. Slowly she made her way to the bank of windows. Staring down at the city, thirty floors below, made her head swim, so she lifted her gaze to the mountains. Cloud-dappled shadows chased each other over the craggy landscape and she stared at them blankly.

She'd been so excited when Dino presented them with this "honeymoon." And so sure of herself and what she wanted to happen between Nick and her while they were here, in this special, isolated world. Now though, her go-for-broke intentions seemed less "go" and more "broke." Where had her sense of reckless adventure disappeared to? One corner of her mouth tilted in a self-mocking smile. Maybe it was the very setting she'd hoped to exploit that was stealing what little courage she had left. Her gaze slid to one side and from the corner of her eye, she noted more of the opulent furnishings.

A shining white, grand piano stood regally in a pool of sunshine as if daring Jenny to lay a finger on its pristine surface. Antique chairs were drawn up to a glass dining table that looked as if it would easily seat twenty people. In the far corner, behind a phalanx of potted ficus trees, was a fully appointed workstation, complete with computer, fax machine and a bank of telephones. She turned her head slightly and looked to the other side of her. A wide-screen television set into the wall stared back at her silently. Alongside it, a complex-looking entertainment system and shelf after shelf filled with CDs and videos.

Jenny groaned quietly and turned back toward the view. What on earth was she doing in a place like this? She was a woman more used to a portable tape player, an occasional glass of beer and a nineteen-inch TV. How had she hoped to fit into this world, even for a few days? And how in heaven was she going to be able to seduce Nick when she was feeling so out of place?

"Nice, huh?"

He'd slipped up behind her so quietly she hadn't heard him approach.

"Uh, yes. It is," she said. Nice? How about flamboyant? Opulent? Intimidating?

"Pretty view."

"Uh-huh."

Good Lord, girl, her mind shouted. *Get a grip, here! Say something. Anything.* ''Where's the bedroom?''

Anything but that.

Jenny blinked and felt a flush crawl up her neck and settle in her cheeks.

Nick's eyebrows lifted, but he jerked his head in the direction of the circular staircase. ''Upstairs. In the loft.''

She nodded. ''I think I'll unpack,'' she said, and squeezed past him, headed for her luggage.

''Good idea.'' He followed right behind her. ''You go on up. I'll bring the bags.''

''Oh. All right.'' Brilliant, she thought. Absolutely scintillating conversation. Scowling at herself, Jenny's mind raced on as she walked to the stairs. She was going to have to do a whole lot better than this to make the weekend everything she'd hoped it would be. For heaven's sake, how was she going to convince him that they had a chance at a *real* marriage if she couldn't even talk to him?

Her fingers curled around the cool, brass handrail and she listened to the sounds of her feet on the steps as she climbed up to the loft.

Nick gritted his teeth and determinedly shifted his gaze to the stairs beneath his feet. If he kept watching the sway of Jenny's hips, he'd forget where he was, tumble down the circular monstrosity and break his fool neck.

At least it would be quick, a voice in his brain whispered. *Better than this dying by inches every day.*

Jenny reached the top of the steps and he heard her gasp. Mentally preparing himself, he hurried up the rest of the way and stopped beside her on the landing. His grip on the bags dissolved and they hit the carpet with a soft thud.

The biggest bed he'd ever seen stretched out in front of them. Dozens of colorful pillows were bunched against the intricately carved wooden headboard and another bottle of iced champagne sat waiting on a small table at the foot of the monster mattress.

He was a dead man.

All of his efforts at keeping his distance from Jenny had brought him to this. The ultimate test. A bed that looked as wide as a stage and a woman whose very presence made him want to forget everything but burying himself inside her.

He groaned inwardly and dutifully shifted his gaze from the bed that demanded his attention. Naturally, he would have liked to think it was big enough to finally allow him to get some sleep. But he had a feeling that even if Jenny was on the other side of the city, she would be able to keep him lying awake and eager.

Pale blue sheers across the wide window let in only diffused sunlight, making the bedroom loft seem shadowy, private. But for the bed and a couple of tables, the loft was unfurnished. There was a walk-in closet on the far wall with built-in drawers and a dressing table complete with oval mirror and makeup lights. An open door on the right no doubt led to the bathroom and Nick didn't even want to think about whatever sensual goodies were hidden in there.

He rubbed his jaw with one hand and let his gaze slip to the woman at his side. Jenny'd been beside herself with excitement only that morning. Now she looked as though she wanted to crawl into a quiet hole somewhere.

She shook her head and walked to the bed where she plopped down onto the edge of the mattress. Her shoulders slumped, she folded her hands in her lap and muttered something he didn't quite catch.

"What?"

She tossed him a quick look, gave him a half smile and shrugged. "I just said that maybe this was a bad idea."

Intrigued at her change of attitude, he started toward her, then caught himself. No sense pushing his luck, he thought. And sitting on that bed, beside her, would definitely be pushing it.

"What changed your mind?" he asked.

"All of this." She waved her hands in the air briefly, encompassing the surrounding luxury. "It's just..." She shook her head again.

"Too much?"

"I guess so." She laughed shortly, then sniffed. "I don't know what I expected, but it sure wasn't this."

Nick felt the same way. Only it wasn't the accommodations surprising him. It was Jenny. He never would have guessed that she would feel so out of place. From what he'd seen, she made herself at home wherever she happened to be. Seeing her like this—so dejected—bothered him more than he wanted to admit.

"Strange, huh?" she asked, and looked up at him again. "Most people would probably love this place."

"Probably," he agreed, though he wasn't one of them. He had never been the showy, flashy type. That was more Dino's style. Funny how both he and Jenny felt the same way about places like this, he told himself.

"I'm almost ashamed to unpack," she went on.

Glancing around the room again, she shuddered slightly, then flopped backward onto the bed. Her legs hung over the edge and her arms were spread wide on either side of her, like a martyred virgin staked out on an altar.

He shifted uncomfortably at the thought.

"You want to know what the funniest part is?" she asked and didn't wait for him to answer. "I was going to seduce you while we were here."

"What?" His groin tightened at the thought and he scowled at his own body's lack of common sense.

She lifted her head off the bed and nodded at him. "That was my plan, anyway." A heavy sigh shot from her as she let her head drop back onto the mattress. "I've never actually seduced anyone on purpose, you know. You would have been my first."

Lucky me, Nick thought on a silent groan.

"I've seen lots of movies and I've read plenty of books," she told him. "So I know what I would have done. But it probably wouldn't have worked."

Wouldn't have worked? Just talking about a seduction had him raring to go. And wondering about what she would have done to seduce him only intensified the throbbing ache within him. He drew one long, shaky breath and looked at her, lying on the bed. Her expression clearly mirrored her disappointment at the way her plan had turned out. When she heaved a sigh, he couldn't help himself. Crossing the space separating them in a few quick strides, he eased down onto the bed, propped himself up on one elbow and, in spite of his better judgment, asked, "Why wouldn't it have worked, Jenny?"

"Oh." She waved one hand at him, but continued to stare up at the ceiling. "You know as well as I do that you're just not interested."

Not interested? His entire body was rock hard and painfully aware of her closeness. Was she blind?

"You haven't even kissed me since the wedding. Except at the party your mother gave us. And that doesn't count, really."

"Why not?" That kiss was still burning on his lips and she said it didn't count?

"Because Dino pushed you into it."

"No, he didn't." Nick Tarantelli did his own kissing in his own sweet time. Nothing his little brother did bothered him one bit. Usually.

"Of course he did." She frowned at him. "You didn't even dance with me until *he* did."

Scowling, Nick flopped over onto his back beside her. All right. She had a point. He *hadn't* liked watching Dino dance with her. And he hadn't much cared for the way every other man in the place had watched her, either. But he'd kissed her because…he gritted his teeth together as the truth roared up in his brain. He'd kissed her because he'd *had* to. He'd needed the taste of her lips and the feel of her body pressed against him as much as he'd needed his next breath.

He threw one arm across his eyes and told himself he'd been without a woman too damned long. That was it. Since Angela, he'd kept pretty much to himself. Oh, he'd dated a few women over the last few years. And God knew Mama had done her best to throw women at him. But he didn't want any part of a relationship that would eventually lead to some sort of commitment or other.

He'd done that. And failed miserably. Apparently, though, he hadn't explained that to Jenny. "It's not that I don't want you," he started to say.

"Oh, please," she interrupted. "I'm not blind."

One eyebrow lifted and he shot her a quick glance. If she took a good look at him right now, she'd see enough hard evidence to convince her to buy herself a white cane and dark glasses.

"I *did* want you," he said, and heard the strangled

tone in his voice. "Hell, I still do. But we didn't get married for real, Jenny. It was a bargain. Something to help you out. Remember?"

"Of course I remember." She frowned but didn't shift her gaze from the ceiling. "Still, a marriage is a marriage."

"No it's not. *This* marriage is ending in a year." He took a long breath and told himself to count to ten. Or twenty, if ten didn't help. When he felt as though he could talk in a reasonable tone again, he continued. "No one said anything about sex, Jenny. It wasn't part of the deal—"

"You don't have to be nice," she cut him off in a rush. She lifted her arms, then let them drop to the mattress again in an expressive, if dramatic, shrug. "Pretending that you were holding yourself back for my sake is just ridiculous. It's obvious to me, you just don't find me attractive. All those nights, laying beside me in a tiny bed and you didn't once react." She sighed heavily and frowned up at the ceiling. "I always thought that the lightning bolt would hit us both when it came."

"Lightning bolt?" His arm fell from his eyes and he turned his head to look at her.

"You remember? I told you about it?"

"Oh, yes." He nodded. Lightning bolts and curses. How could he forget?

She sniffed again and his eyes narrowed. Was she going to cry? Lord, he hoped not.

"Well, when I felt it, I thought you had, too, so

naturally, I wanted to make this a real marriage and so I thought that if I was to seduce you, then you would see things the way I do and then you would realize that it was a blessing and not a curse that brought us together and then we could—''

Her babbling broke off abruptly and Nick winced as a single tear rolled down her cheek and dropped onto the silk coverlet beneath them. She sniffed again, rubbed her eyes with the back of her hand, then pressed her lips together tightly in a futile effort to bring her rampant emotions under control.

"I shouldn't be crying," she said stiffly. "You're a nice man and you helped me when no one else would. You saved my grandmother's life for heaven's sake." She sniffed, then went on, softer this time. Another tear slid down the curve of her cheek. "It's not your fault that you don't want me."

Nick reached for her, intending only to comfort her. Hold her until those blasted tears stopped and he could think clearly again. But she rolled into the circle of his arms, buried her face in his chest and hugged him tight. His hands moved up and down her back in a slow, rhythmic caress.

Curling up into him, she drew her right knee up and brushed across his groin.

He groaned.

She gasped, tilted her head back and stared at him through blue eyes shining with pleasure. "Is that for me?"

"You see anybody else in here?"

He felt her heart thundering against his and when she slowly shook her head, he lowered his mouth to hers.

The moment their lips met, a flash of something white-hot and dangerous rushed through him. But he was beyond caring about what he should and shouldn't do. He deepened the kiss, opening her mouth with his tongue and sweeping inside to taste the sweet warmth of her.

She moaned softly and the sound tore through him, enflaming his own desires until he felt as though his body was on fire. This is what he needed, he thought wildly. Jenny. Her mouth. Her touch. Like a drowning man finally pulled to safety, he held on to her as if she meant his life. One hand slid to her bottom and held her against his hard, aching flesh. Pressure increased and an all-consuming desire burst in his chest like a skyrocket, sending splinters of heat to every corner of his body.

On a muffled oath, he abruptly broke the kiss. He staggered to his feet and pulled Jenny up beside him. She wobbled unsteadily and leaned into him for support. Holding her upright with one hand, he yanked the silken quilt off the bed, then pulled the neatly arranged sheets and blankets back out of his way.

Finally, he turned to her. Cupping her shoulders with his palms, he said, "Now's the time to say so, if you've changed your mind about this."

Her tongue darted out to lick suddenly dry lips. Jenny looked up into his dark brown gaze and saw the flash of the lightning bolt. Whether he admitted it or not, he felt it. She *knew* he did. His touch was everything she'd ever dreamed of. His kiss was more than she'd ever hoped for. And she wanted to know the rest.

She wanted it all.

He was waiting for an answer and suddenly she couldn't find her voice. But words weren't needed. Instinct told her what to do. She reached for the oversize, yellow plastic buttons on her bright white dress and began to undo them. Clumsy at first, her fingers began to move more quickly as if feeding on her eagerness.

Nick jerked her a nod, then began to tug at his own clothes. She watched as he pulled his pale green knit shirt over his head. His chest was hard, muscled and so broad, she couldn't keep herself from reaching out to caress him. He groaned, caught her hand in his and planted a kiss in the palm.

Reluctantly, he let her go then, and in seconds their clothes were jumbled together in a heap on the floor. Nick swept her up in his arms, knelt on the bed and laid her down gently in the center of the mattress. She watched him as he slowly lowered himself over her. She felt the brush of his skin against hers and marveled at the heat radiating from him.

Nick dipped his head to claim her mouth in a quick kiss, then shifted to drag his lips and tongue along the line of her throat. Jenny gasped and tipped her head back against the bed, giving him easier access.

Every teasing stroke of his tongue raised a new crop of goose bumps to fly across her skin.

She shivered expectantly as his right hand shifted to explore the curves and valleys of her body. When his palm grazed the tip of her erect nipple, she jerked in response.

He lifted his head from her throat and smiled down at her briefly before moving to take that sensitive bud into his mouth. She gasped and reached for him. In a suddenly rocking world, she clutched at his shoulders as if for support.

His tongue made warm, damp circles around her distended flesh, while his right hand swept down across her ribcage, over her abdomen to cup the very heart of her. Her hips twisted against the silk sheets as she tried desperately to move against his hand. And when he began to suckle at her breast, her back arched high, silently asking for more.

She didn't know how to move. She didn't know which part of her body ached more desperately. All she knew for certain was that she didn't want him to stop. She concentrated on the feel of his hands, the damp heat of his tongue, the rigid strength of his sex, pressing against her hip.

Nick lifted his head and watched her face as he slowly dipped one finger into her damp heat, then withdrew to caress the tiny, hard nub at the apex of her thighs. Her eyes widened and she lifted her hips again, seeking...needing more.

"Are you seducing me now, Jenny?" he whispered, and bent to brush a gentle kiss across her mouth.

"I don't think so," she gasped, then groaned as he once more dipped into her body, this time filling her with two fingers.

"You're wrong," Nick told her and stared at her as if seeing her for the first time. "Every breath, every moan of pleasure you make, seduces me again and again."

Jenny looked up at him through passion-glazed eyes and believed him. He looked as tormented as she felt. Letting one hand slide from the back of his neck, her fingertips grazed across the mat of curly brown hair covering the middle of his chest. His flesh jumped beneath her touch and when she skimmed across one of his flattened nipples, his head fell back.

Smiling inwardly at the knowledge that he wanted her as badly as she did him, she continued with her exploring until her fingers curled around his thick, hard shaft. At her touch, he sucked in a gulp of air and moved to kneel between her parted thighs.

His fingers caressed her most intimate flesh and she began to move restlessly, hungrily under his touch. Fire blossomed deep inside her and she felt a need like she had never known before. Arching her hips helplessly, she whispered, "Please, Nick. Please."

He dipped one finger into her warmth and as he caressed the slick heat of her, he asked, "Is it safe?"

"What?"

"Safe, Jenny," he repeated through gritted teeth. "Is it safe for us to go ahead?"

"Yes." She nodded and licked her dry lips. "I'm safe."

He silently prayed up to heaven in relief.

Cupping her bottom, he gently prodded and then tenderly pushed his way into her depths. You're so tight, Jenny. So good."

A soft moan escaped her as her body adjusted to his presence. Then he began the slow, heated dance they'd both waited for. She wrapped her legs around him, dug her fingers into his shoulders and when the first tremor shook her, she cried his name. Pleasure was still rippling through her body when Nick arched against her, groaned and gave her everything he had to give.

Nine

Jenny ran the flat of her hand over Nick's chest then let her palm glide down his tanned flesh and across his abdomen. As her fingers lightly stroked the inside of his thigh, his eyes flew open.

"Good morning," she said, and bent to kiss him.

He reacted quickly, flipping her over onto her back and propping himself up on one elbow to look down at her. He gave her the kiss she'd sought, then lifted his head and smiled. "Don't you ever sleep?"

"I'm not tired at all," she told him, and to prove it, ran her hand down his body again.

He laughed shortly. "Beds are for sleeping, too, you know."

"We can sleep anytime."

"We haven't yet," he reminded her with a half laugh.

A satisfied smile curved her lips. After three days of precious little sleep, she felt wonderful. Energized.

"Sleep is very overrated," she told him as her fingers curled around the rigid length of him.

Nick sucked in a gulp of air through gritted teeth. "Jenny..."

"Be inside me again, Nick." She half rose and began to nibble at his throat. "Once more before we have to leave here."

He didn't need any urging. He dipped his head to slowly take one of her erect nipples into his mouth. He rolled his tongue around the sensitive tip and smiled to himself when she arched into him.

Her fingers continued to stroke and caress him, filling him with a driving need to claim this woman as he had all weekend. Again and again, he had buried himself inside her, hoping each time to ease the hunger for her. But each time with her was like the first time. Each thrust into her warmth only increased his need.

His left hand smoothed down her body and across her flat belly to the damp heat of her center. She lifted her hips in silent invitation and her thighs parted, welcoming him home. He dipped one finger inside her and groaned at the feel of her hot, wet flesh closing around him.

And it wasn't enough.

He needed more. He needed to taste her. To touch

her so intimately that a part of her soul would always be with him.

He straightened, ignored her soft moan of protest and moved to kneel between her parted thighs. Slipping his palms beneath her bottom, he lifted her hips from the mattress.

"Nick?" She reached for him, but he shook his head.

"Lift your legs onto my shoulders," he told her.

She twisted her hips in his grasp instead as realization dawned in her eyes. "Nick, I..."

"It's all right," he told her. "Just do it."

Squeezing her eyes shut, she did as he asked. He saw her dig her fingers into the silk sheets and tighten her grip until her knuckles were white.

Then he lowered his mouth to claim the small, hard bud of her sex. She gasped and jerked in his arms, but he held her still as his tongue slowly began to stroke that most sensitive piece of flesh.

Jenny tried to catch her breath, but couldn't. Her heartbeat thundered in her ears. She could feel her blood racing through her veins and her entire body turned to fire in the sensual heat he gave her. She opened her eyes and watched him as he loved her.

She should be shaking with embarrassment. But she wasn't. Instead, an incredible delight spiraled through her. And with it, came the aching that was becoming so familiar to her. Gasping for air, she found herself straining toward completion. As his mouth and tongue tortured her sweetly, she groaned and reached for him. The fire inside her was so much stronger this time. So much bigger. She wanted—no, *needed*—his body joined with hers when she found that brief, soul-shattering peace.

"Nick, please," she whispered brokenly. "I need to feel you inside me. A part of me."

His groan echoed hers as he reluctantly lay her back down and moved to cover her with his body. But she shifted position, coaxed him onto his back and straddled his hips.

Slowly then, she lowered herself onto his shaft.

By inches, she took him into her body.

"Ah, Jenny," he whispered as his length was finally fully within her heat.

He held her hips tightly and as she began to move on him, she felt the hard, strong length of him reach up and touch her soul. Rocking her body back and forth, her hands braced on either side of his head, she released him only to capture him again. Slowly, deeply, she stroked him. Sitting straight, she arched her back and ground her hips against his until the sharp, tingling sensation inside her erupted into a frenzy of feeling. She shouted his name as the last of the tremors whipped through her, then she watched his face as his own release came a moment later. His hips bucked beneath her and a strangled cry burst from his throat. A heartbeat later he grabbed her, pulling her down to his chest and she went limp, burying her face in the crook of his neck.

Incredible. Nick stared up at the ceiling, listened to

his own tortured breathing and tried to quiet his racing heart. He wrapped his arms tight around Jenny and knew that he would never again be as completely at peace as he was at that moment.

Their bodies still locked together, he told himself to remember. To remember everything about this remarkable weekend with his temporary wife. Over the last few days, he'd tried to tell himself that it was just sex. That the attraction and desire he felt for this woman was simply a matter of chemistry. Attraction. Lust.

But it was more than that. So much more it terrified him.

Sex wasn't a big enough word to describe what happened when the two of them came together. Sex was simply two people scratching an itch.

Making love with Jenny was exactly that. Making love.

For the first time in his life, he understood why it was called *making love*. Every touch of her hand. Every kiss. Every breathy sigh left an indelible mark on him.

In the last three days, they'd come together more times than he could count. And each time was different. Each time better than the last. Each climax harder, stronger, more satisfying than anything he'd ever experienced.

And once they left this place, it could never happen again.

He frowned at the ceiling and let his right hand

trail regretfully down the line of her spine. He couldn't allow himself to touch her again. Because if he did, he knew instinctively he would never want to let her go.

Determinedly, he rolled her onto her side and reluctantly slipped his body free of hers. Then he moved quickly to sit on the edge of the bed, as far from her tempting self as he could get without leaving the room.

"Nick?"

He glanced at her over his shoulder and saw the questions in her eyes. The hurt. The surprise. But as he stared into those shining blue eyes, he saw something else, as well. Something that steeled him against giving in to the urge to drive himself into her again.

In Jenny's eyes, he saw white picket fences. He saw dreams.

He saw the faces of his unborn children.

Leaping off the bed, he walked to the bathroom, only a few steps away. Giving the gold-handled faucet a quick turn, he bent over and splashed cold water on his face and neck.

"Are you all right?" Jenny called.

Hell, no! He'd just looked into a woman's eyes and seen a future that he'd tried to avoid for years. He might never be all right again.

Out loud, though, he said only, "Yeah. I just want to take a shower, that's all."

"Good idea."

His head fell forward until his forehead was

pressed against the cool glass of the mirror. Unbidden, memories of the shower they'd taken together the night before rushed into his brain. He never would have guessed that there was that much room in a shower stall. Or that there were so many uses for a shower massage.

He groaned quietly.

"Nick?"

Straightening, he looked into the mirror and met Jenny's concerned gaze. With the silk quilt wrapped around her like some luxurious toga, she looked more alluring than she had stark naked.

He was never going to survive this.

"What's wrong?"

Everything. "Nothing," he said.

She took a step into the room then stumbled into him when her quilt caught on something behind her. Tilting her head back, she grinned up at him. "Sorry. I guess the high heels don't have much to do with if I fall over or not."

Carefully but firmly, he set her back from him and took a half step away.

"What's going on?"

He inhaled sharply and pushed one hand through his hair. "Jenny, this isn't going to work."

"What?"

"This." He waved one hand at her, then at himself. "You. Me. Us."

"I thought it was working wonderfully well," she said, and gave him a slow, satisfied smile.

Too well, he told himself, curling his fingers around the sink edge to keep from grabbing her. "Look, Jenny," he forced himself to say. "This weekend was…"

"Terrific?"

"Nice," he amended, and silently snorted at the inappropriate word.

"Nice." She frowned, crossed her arms over her chest and waited, watching his face in the mirror.

"But it's over. We have to go back to reality now and there's no place for all of this in our reality."

"You mean, there's no place for us in *your* reality."

"Yeah. I guess that's what I mean."

She stepped closer and grabbed his forearm. "Why are you doing this? What happened between us was special. You know it was."

He sucked in another long breath and forced himself to keep from reaching out for her. "It was great, Jenny. But let's not fool ourselves, okay? This is a temporary marriage, with an even more temporary honeymoon."

"It doesn't have to be that way."

"Yes, it does."

"Why don't you even want to *talk* about the possibility of more?"

Nick splashed a bit more cold water on his face, raked it back through his hair, then turned off the faucet. Meeting her gaze in the mirror, he spoke stiffly. "I tried marriage once before." Grimacing at the rush of memories, he added. "Trust me. I was a lousy husband."

"A marriage takes two people to make it work."

"Some people just shouldn't be married."

"That's ridiculous." She smiled, but the smile faded as he continued to stare at her.

"No, it's not. My marriage was a disaster."

"Dino told me about your wife."

Nick snorted a choked laugh. "Did he tell you that because of me, my mother hasn't seen her youngest son in five years?"

She shook her head. "All he said was that Angela ran away with your brother."

"*All?*" he rasped. "Isn't that enough? I hurt my whole damn family by failing at something I had no business trying in the first place."

"You didn't hurt them. Angela and Tony did."

"No, damn it!" His shout seemed to echo in the cavernous bathroom and he took a long moment to get himself under control again. "It was my failure that caused Angela to turn to Tony. And it was because of me that Tony felt he couldn't stay here in Vegas."

"Nick—"

"I'm just not husband material, Jenny. Face it."

"Did you love Angela?" She whispered her question as if afraid of the answer.

Love Angela? He'd thought he had. But the feelings he'd had for Angela were nothing like what shook through him whenever Jenny was near. Hell.

He didn't know anymore. He didn't know a damned thing. All he was certain of was that he had to stay away from Jenny for both their sakes.

"I don't know," he sighed. "I thought so."

"This time is different," she said quickly, tightening her hold on his arm. "You felt it. I know you did."

"Felt what?"

"The lightning bolt."

"God, Jenny..."

"You did!" She yanked him around to face her. Tilting her head way back, she poked her index finger at his chest and dared him to deny it. "You felt the magic between us. I saw it in your eyes. I felt it in your touch."

He looked deeply into her eyes and told the biggest lie of his life. "I didn't feel any magic. There *is* no magic. Just like there *is* no curse."

To his relief, he didn't see tears forming in her startlingly blue eyes. He'd rather have her mad as hell at him than crying. If she cried, it would kill him.

"Why are you doing this?" she whispered. "Why are you shutting me out?"

"I'm only doing what we agreed to when we got married." He rubbed one hand across his jaw viciously. "I'm keeping the bargain."

"The bargain." She nodded slowly, then let her gaze slide down his body, stopping when she saw that he was hard and ready for her again. Glancing back up into his eyes, she said, "You may think you're doing the right thing, but the rest of you disagrees."

"Jenny!" he snapped. "A man would have to be dead not to get turned on around you. It doesn't mean a damn thing!"

She blanched as if he'd struck her. Nick wanted to snatch his words back, but it was too late. He was a real bastard. Too bad she didn't believe that he was trying to do her a favor here.

"I'm just not the right man for you." He tried again, more calmly this time. "Hell, Jenny. I didn't even bring a condom with me on this 'honeymoon.' If you hadn't been safe already, I might've made you pregnant. Then where would we be?"

She suddenly looked even paler.

Uneasiness trickled through him.

"Jenny?"

"What?"

"You *did* say it was safe, right?"

She chewed at her bottom lip, then lifted one hand to cover her mouth. Her gaze slipped away from his. "That's what you meant?"

That trickle of unease widened into a swiftly moving stream.

"Yes. What did you think I meant?"

She lifted her shoulders and pushed one hand through her hair. Still looking down at her feet, she said, "I thought you meant...you know, *diseases*."

"Oh, God." Nick tilted his head back and stared

straight up at the ceiling as if waiting to be struck blind.

"So I said I was safe, because you're the first, really. I mean the only other man I ever...was Patrick Ryan and we were only eighteen at the time. And well..." She paused and shook her head. "He doesn't actually count, after all."

"What?" Nick lifted his head and looked down at her.

"He was very young and—" she shrugged again "—well, the spirit was willing, but..."

Well, hell, this just got better and better. She'd been practically a virgin and he had acted completely irresponsibly. Whatever happened, he deserved it. But Jenny didn't. She was the inexperienced one.

And no poor, innocent baby deserved *him* for a father.

"How long until we'll know if you're pregnant?" he asked.

Lifting her chin slightly, she said, "Don't worry about it, Nick. I can take care of myself."

"This concerns both of us, Jenny."

"We don't know that yet."

He wanted to say more, but what else was there to say? Disgusted with himself, he lifted one hand and rubbed his tired eyes with his fingertips. Now all they could do was wait. And hope for the best.

Silently she turned away from him and swept out of the bathroom. He watched as the door swung softly closed behind her.

A cold hand gripped his heart and bands of steel tightened around his chest, crushing him. In the silence of the room, he suddenly felt more alone than ever before. Nick swiveled his head to look at his reflection.

"You'd better hope to heaven there's no baby," he said grimly. Although briefly, he allowed himself to imagine what it would be like to smooth his hand over Jenny's belly and feel their child respond with a kick.

No.

It was better this way. Better for her. Better for him. She'd see. One day, Jenny would look back to this moment and thank him for being strong enough to turn his back on her.

"Strong enough?" he muttered to the fool in the mirror. "Or stupid enough?"

The man was a fool, Jenny told herself. A complete and utter fool.

She marched across the bedroom to the windows. Holding on to the quilt still wrapped around her with one hand, she yanked back the draperies with the other and stared out at the desert morning.

Deeply stung by his hurtful words, she wanted to strangle Nick. But it wouldn't have changed anything. He was just stubborn enough to draw his last breath still claiming that he knew best.

She glanced over her shoulder at the closed bathroom door. He'd been deliberately mean, in an effort to make her so angry she'd forget about wanting him. And his words *had* stung. But not as badly as the realization that he was willing to walk away from what they might find together.

Well, he could pretend or lie all he wanted to. She would never believe that he hadn't felt the lightning bolt. He was the man she'd waited for most of her life and she sure wasn't about to give up on him without a fight. She'd left everything behind her when she'd come to Las Vegas to find a husband. She'd thrown away her secretarial job, her apartment, her friends—everything that was familiar and safe—in an effort to save her grandmother.

Now, Grandma Tess was in no danger and Jenny was left with a husband who couldn't see the truth when it reared up and looked him dead in the eye.

Scowling, she turned back to stare at the distant mountains. Twenty-seven years she'd waited for that blasted lightning bolt. Wouldn't you know that when it finally arrived, it would point the way to the one man who didn't have the sense to claim it!

She'd stored up a lot of dreams while waiting, too. And she wanted those dreams. Images she'd nourished all through her lonely childhood.

A family of her own.

A husband who loved her.

A houseful of kids.

She wanted to *belong*. To be *needed*.

Unconsciously, she laid the flat of her hand on her belly. Was there a child already growing inside her?

A small smile curved her lips. Perhaps she shouldn't be pleased at the possibility, but she couldn't help it. Besides, if they *had* made a baby together, at least *one* of them should want the child.

Jenny inhaled sharply, dropped the draperies back into place and turned around to face that blasted door. He would have to come out sometime, she told herself. And when he did, no doubt he would be just as surly as he could manage.

Well, it was going to take more than *that* to chase her off. Like it or not, he was her husband. And if Nick thought *he* could be stubborn, he hadn't seen Jenny Blake Tarantelli when she dug in her heels.

Ten

A few days later Jenny sat at a booth in Tarantelli's Terrace, pretending to eat lasagna. The restaurant was crowded, as usual, but the hustle and noise of the crowd barely reached her. She'd gone to the restaurant looking for help. But now that she was there, she was having a hard time bringing up the subject. It almost felt disloyal talking to Nick's mother about their problems.

On the other hand, she thought wryly, what choice did she have? Jenny sighed and poked her fork at the lasagna on her plate.

"Mangia," Mama told her in Italian first, then translated. "Eat. You're too skinny."

"Leave her alone, Ma." Gina laughed and speared

another forkful of Caesar salad. Glancing at her sister-in-law, the dark-eyed beauty confided, "If you eat every time Mama tells you to, you'll weigh five hundred pounds by the end of the year."

Clearly, Gina paid no attention to her mother's coaxing. Nick's sister was tall, slender, and very elegant-looking in a tailored, pale green business suit.

Mama scowled at her daughter, waved her comments away with one hand, then turned to Jenny. "So. You gonna tell me what's wrong or you gonna make me guess?"

Jenny lifted her gaze to Nick's mother. The woman didn't miss much, that was for sure. But then, that was exactly why Jenny had come to her.

Since leaving the hotel and their too brief honeymoon behind them, Jenny and Nick had lived like two warring nations under an armed truce. Her husband was polite, considerate and, on the rare occasions he was at their small house, far too distant.

She'd hoped that the day-to-day living together would wear him down. Make him see that they could be wonderful together. But he was proving to be far more stubborn than she'd thought. Finally, she'd decided to go to his mother for information. Jenny only hoped she wouldn't hurt the older woman too badly with her questions about Nick's ex-wife, Angela, and Tony.

Stopping by the restaurant at lunchtime, Jenny had been pleased to find Gina there, as well. At this point, she needed all the help she could get.

"Jeez, Ma," Gina said. "Does something *have* to be wrong?"

"No, Miss Lawyer Person," Mama countered. "But something *is* wrong, isn't there?"

Staring into those warm brown eyes, Jenny couldn't have lied even if she'd wanted to. Which she didn't. Slowly, she nodded.

"Ah-ha!" Mama shot one triumphant look at her daughter, then reached out to pat Jenny's hand. "What is it? You can tell me. What did Nicky do?"

Jenny blinked. "He didn't *do* anything."

Mama frowned. "So what is it?"

Gina set her fork down quietly and watched Jenny. "Are you all right?"

"Yes. No." She shook her head. "I suppose so. I mean, I'm not sick or anything."

"Pregnant, maybe?" Mama's eyebrows lifted hopefully.

"Ma!"

"No," Jenny said quickly, hoping to avoid one of the long, involved Tarantelli "discussions." "I'm not pregnant." At least, she didn't think so. Of course, during those few days at the Taj, she and Nick had certainly upped her chances. Briefly, she considered the possibility. And as much as she would love to have Nick's baby—she'd rather find herself pregnant by choice than by happenstance. But the way things stood now, it didn't look promising. "In fact," she whispered, more to herself than anyone else, "the way things are going, I never will be."

"Ahhh...." Mama nodded sagely, then frowned.

Jenny winced, surprised that she'd voiced her feelings out loud.

"What's the matter with Nicky?" her mother-in-law demanded. "And you such a beautiful girl! Don't you worry, Jenny," she said firmly. "*I'll* have a talk with him."

"Oh, no," Jenny practically shouted, then quickly looked around at the interested faces of the patrons turning toward her. Ducking her head slightly, she said, "Don't do that, Mama. Please."

"Somebody's got to do it."

"Jeez, Ma," Gina leaned closer and whispered, "Nick doesn't need a lecture on the facts of life from his mommy!"

"What? You didn't hear Jenny?"

"That's not what I meant," Jenny broke in and silently congratulated herself. She was learning how to interrupt and be heard.

"So what did you mean?"

There was no way to do this but bluntly. Honestly. Jenny took a deep, calming breath and blurted it out.

"Nick says he doesn't want this marriage to last. He's determined to end it when a year is up, just like we agreed."

"And you don't want it to?" Gina asked softly.

"No," Jenny admitted. "I love him."

"Good!" Mama clapped her hands together and when a customer turned a scowl on her, she told him, "Mind your own business. *Mangia.* Eat."

"Is that bad? Loving Nick, I mean?"

"Of course it's not bad." Mama froze her daughter with a look, then patted Jenny's hand again. "You and my Nicky will be good for each other. You'll see."

"I know that," Jenny said. "It's Nick who doesn't want to see it."

"Why not?" Mama demanded.

"He says he makes a lousy husband. He says it's because of him that you don't get to see your youngest son anymore."

Mama sucked in a breath and Gina's gaze shot to her.

"Ma?"

"It's all right," the older woman nodded slowly. "I'm fine." Looking directly at Jenny, Mama asked, "My idiot son? What does he say about Angela and Tony?"

Grateful that Mama didn't seem to mind talking about all this, Jenny said. "He didn't say much. Only that he failed Angela and that she ran away with Tony because Nick couldn't be a good husband. He blames himself for Tony disappearing and for your pain."

Mama nodded, waved away Gina's consoling hand, then reached up to unnecessarily smooth her impeccable topknot.

"Nicky," she muttered, shaking her head. "Always, he was like this. Even as a little boy, Nicky thought it was up to him to take care of everybody. He used to be the police, you know," Mama said softly. "He likes to help people. He's a good boy, my Nicky."

Jenny nodded. She already knew that Nick had helped raise his brothers and sister. And she'd seen for herself what kind of man he was. A wistful smile crossed her face as she realized that Nick, whether he knew it or not, was the kind of man who not only accepted responsibility—he went out looking for it.

He'd been a police officer, no doubt as his mother had said, to help people. As a bounty hunter, she'd noticed that the criminals Nick went after were generally abusive husbands or fathers. Men who failed to pay child support. Or, Jenny told herself, men like Jimmy the Lip Baldini, who married women and then left them. Even in his work, Nick continued looking out for people who couldn't speak up for themselves.

The best example of that was herself. Hadn't he married a perfect stranger just to keep her grandmother safe?

"Oh, Nicky was always one to worry for everything," Mama said. "But this?" The older woman sighed, picked up Jenny's hand and squeezed it between both of her own. "*Nobody* could make Angela happy," she said softly. "That woman." Her gaze narrowed and Jenny would have sworn she saw sparks shooting out of Mama's eyes. "Always wanting something. Always complaining. Buy me this. Get me that. Why don't you talk to me? Why don't you stay home with me?" Mama snorted. "What? A man's not supposed to work? He's supposed to stay at home trying to please a woman who won't be pleased?''

"Angela," Gina interrupted, then continued at her mother's nod, "was a clinging, demanding woman. Nothing Nick did was good enough. I never did see why he married her in the first place."

"Ha!" Mama shouted, then settled down. "I can tell you that. Because he took a look at Angela and stopped thinking with his brain."

Jenny nodded. She could almost understand. Her own hormones went into overdrive every time she saw Nick.

"Anyway," Gina said firmly, "he *did* marry her. It didn't last long, though. When Nick didn't give her the constant attention and compliments she expected, she turned to Tony."

"Two sons she ruined," Mama whispered. "And one she stole from me. She better not ever show her lying face around here again. I would put such a curse on her...."

Jenny took one look at the promise in Mama's eyes and believed her.

"Tony was young. And stupid," Gina finished. "He ran off with her and by now, he's probably too ashamed to come back."

"Do you think they're still together?" Jenny asked.

Mama snorted. "That woman was not made to be a wife. No, by now, she has left my Tony, too. Where, I don't know." She fell silent for a long moment and her eyes took on a faraway look. Then abruptly, she shrugged her shoulders as if ridding herself of a heavy burden before asking Jenny, "You say Nicky blames himself for Tony being gone?"

"Yes."

"I'll have a talk with him," she promised.

"Don't do that, Mama," Jenny pleaded. "Then Nick will know I came to ask you about this. I'd rather he didn't."

The older woman frowned, then glanced at her daughter, who nodded firmly. At last, Mama agreed. "All right. But you should know something, Jenny."

"What's that?"

Mama grinned. "My Nicky, he got his good looks from me. But that stubborn will of his, he got from his papa, God rest his soul." She crossed herself, then winked at Gina. "But you remember? Your papa, he had a hard head. Like a rock. But still, he could listen. He could admit when he was wrong."

"I remember, Ma."

"Nicky's like that, too." The older woman squeezed Jenny's hand again. "You'll see. Nicky will understand how he's being foolish and everything will be fine."

Jenny smiled and nodded, even though she was far from feeling as confident as Mama.

"And once we get this all straightened out, you'll start making me some grandbabies, huh?"

"Ma!"

If Angela was a clinging, demanding wife, then Jenny needed to prove to Nick just how different she was from that woman. She had to show him that as much as she wanted to be with him—she would be able to survive without him.

The first step in doing that, she told herself, was to get a job. Besides, she thought with a smile, she was getting tired of staying around the house anyway. Especially now that Nick was spending as little time as possible there.

She stepped out of the cab, paid the driver and started up the flower-lined walk to her front door. Maybe she should see about getting a car first. Surely she'd be able to find a cheap used car somewhere in Las Vegas. Of course, she could ask Nick for help in finding one. But, she thought with a determined smile, it would be better if she simply took care of it on her own.

At the porch, she paused long enough to grab up the mail before unlocking the front door and stepping into the air-conditioned coolness. From force of habit, Jenny rifled through the stack of envelopes. Not that she expected to find anything for her, but you never knew.

She stopped when she saw her name scrawled in a familiar hand. Grandma Tess.

Setting down her purse and the rest of the mail on the closest table, Jenny ripped open the envelope and tore out the single sheet of paper inside.

"Hon," it said. "Coming for a quick visit. Have to meet my new grandson. Should be there on the fifteenth. Can't wait to see you again. Hugs, Tess."

Her new grandson. Jenny chewed thoughtfully at her bottom lip. As delighted as she was by the prospect of seeing her grandmother again, she couldn't help wondering just how Nick and Grandma Tess would get along. Tess had never been known for her tact and diplomacy. And Nick was walking around like a grizzly bear with a sore paw.

She was almost sorry she didn't already *have* a job. At least then she'd be out of the house for eight hours a day. In the next instant, she dismissed her worries. Grandma Tess never stayed long when she came to town. Usually, it was one or two days and she was off again to some new corner of the globe. Well, Jenny decided, she was going to enjoy Tess's visit. She would get a job the moment her grandmother left town. That would be soon enough.

Glancing back at the letter in her hand, Jenny frowned. The fifteenth? Tomorrow! That was like Tess, too. Not one for plans, Jenny's grandmother lived life on the spur of the moment and expected everyone else to adapt.

Grinning, she started for the kitchen. Grandma Tess would be expecting her favorite homemade cinnamon rolls.

Nick lifted his drink, took another sip of beer and frowned as the cold brew slid down his throat. Setting down the bottle on the cloth-covered table, he never took his gaze off the couple on the dance floor.

Grandmother?

He snorted.

Tess O'Reilly Blake was like no grandmother *he'd* ever seen. Nick had been expecting to meet a frail old woman, with skin like parchment, a shaky voice and watery eyes. He'd been prepared to help the old lady maneuver around in her orthopedic shoes and had even memorized the phone number to the local emergency room.

Boy, what a fool he was.

Dino began an intricate turn, spinning his partner across the floor in a flurry of movement that sent Grandma Tess's skirt flying high above her knees.

Nick scowled again. At least now he knew where Jenny had gotten her great legs. She'd inherited them from the trim, athletic woman laughing up into Dino's smiling features.

Grandma Tess insisted she was "well over seventy," but she didn't look more than fifty. And Nick was willing to bet that if the woman had dyed her elegantly styled, snow-white hair, she could have passed for forty.

Grumbling slightly, Nick shifted his gaze from Dino and Tess to another couple. Jenny was dancing with Nick's former partner on the force, Dan Heredia, who was actually Gina's date for the evening. And from what Nick could see, Dan's proprietary grip on Jenny was a bit too friendly.

But then, what did he care? It wasn't as if Jenny owed him anything. Hell, the way he'd been acting lately, he wouldn't have blamed her if she'd just packed up her bags and said the hell with it. He reached for his beer again as he told himself she would never do that. She was too worried about endangering her poor old grandmother's life.

Poor old grandma, right. The only danger facing Tess was that of exhaustion from too much dancing.

The old Glenn Miller tune ended and the couples began to drift off the floor toward the tables. Gritting his teeth, Nick waited for his dinner companions to rejoin him.

Dan and Jenny reached the table first.

"Thank you," she said.

"My pleasure," Dan grinned, then turned to Gina as another record began. "How about it? Once around the floor?"

"Delighted, Officer," Gina stood and slipped her hand into Dan's.

As they walked away, Jenny commented. "Your friend's a wonderful dancer."

She looked fantastic. Her dark red dress hugged her figure and the deep V neckline displayed to advantage the breasts he ached to touch again. It was pure torture to sit opposite her and know that he couldn't have her. That he would never be inside her again.

"Too bad you didn't marry him." Even as he said it, Nick wanted to kick himself. Hell, he was only mad because his pants, which were getting tighter by the minute, were making him so damned uncomfortable.

"Maybe it is," she said quietly.

For some reason, *that* statement infuriated him. It didn't matter that she had every reason to be furious at him. It didn't matter that he'd been telling himself for days that they never should have married. In fact *nothing* mattered except Jenny's bald statement that she should have married someone else.

"It's never too late," he growled. "Vegas has just as many divorces as marriages you know."

"I'll keep it in mind." Her usually smiling blue eyes were shooting bullets of ice at him. If looks could kill, they'd be planting flowers atop Nick at that very moment.

"And how are my two favorite lovebirds?" Tess asked as Dino settled her in her chair, then headed toward the bar.

Neither of them answered and the stoney silence threatened to go on forever until Tess spoke up again.

"All right," she demanded. "Let's have it."

"Have what?" Jenny turned suddenly innocent eyes on her grandmother.

"Stow it, Jenny. I've known you too long and too well." Tess eyed her granddaughter fiercely, then turned that same glare on Nick. "One of you is going to tell me what's going on around here. And you're going to tell me now."

Eleven

"That is," Tess said when Jenny finished talking, "without a doubt, the silliest thing I have ever heard."

Nick grinned and nodded at Jenny. Who would have thought it would be her own grandmother to step right up and call this curse business the nonsense it was?

"Tess," Jenny countered quickly, with barely a glance at her husband. "Don't you remember Great-great-aunt Penelope?"

The older woman frowned, took a sip of beer and asked, "What about her?"

Nick almost groaned. He should have known that Jenny wouldn't give up so easily.

"When I was a girl," she started to explain, leaning toward her grandmother with an earnest, worried expression on her face, "Mother told me about Aunt Penelope. And about what happened when she didn't take the curse seriously."

"Your mother," Tess said firmly but kindly, "was not the most rational of women."

"Maybe not, but she said that Aunt Bernice had told her the story."

Tess snorted.

Nick frowned. If this Bernice was too much for Tess to handle…he never wanted to meet her.

"Anyway, Aunt Penelope wasn't married on her twenty-seventh birthday." Jenny flashed Nick a quick look, then turned back to her grandmother. "She said that she wouldn't let some curse nonsense saddle her with a husband she didn't want."

"Sensible woman," Tess muttered.

"But the morning of her twenty-seventh birthday," Jenny went on, "Penelope's grandmother Hortensia was run over by an ice wagon!"

"Doesn't prove a thing," Tess told her sharply. "Hortensia was a secret drinker." Nodding at Nick, she confided. "Claimed brandy soothed her rheumatism, as I recall. Although, she always seemed able to walk to the closest saloon."

"Grandmother!"

"Jenny." Tess reached out and caught her granddaughter's hand in hers. "I appreciate what you tried to do. Really." Her eyes narrowed slightly as she continued. "But the idea of you two marrying to keep me alive is ludicrous."

Even though he'd said practically the same thing just before their wedding, Nick couldn't help feeling sorry for Jenny. Tess might have been a bit more diplomatic about the whole thing. After all, her granddaughter had married a stranger, just to protect *her*.

Straightening in her chair, the older woman eyed the two younger people for a long moment. "I'll tell you right now, I have no intention of dying for another twenty or thirty years. And whether you two stay married or not has nothing to do with it." She shifted her gaze to Nick. "I like you, boy. You seem a good sort and you've got a terrific family. Jenny could have done worse."

"Thanks."

"But this marriage of yours is between you and my granddaughter. Don't drag me or anyone else into it."

"Wasn't planning to," he assured her, and told himself that he could get used to having Tess around more often. The woman had plenty of common sense.

"Now," she said as she pushed away from the table and stood. "I'm going to the kitchen to try to talk Marianna into coming out here to sit down for a while. Busiest woman I ever met." Tess winked at Jenny and reached down to stroke her cheek. "Then I'm going to go find that brother-in-law of yours and coerce him into dancing with me again."

Jenny's obviously forced smile tore at Nick's insides.

She looked as if she'd had a rug pulled out from under her. And in a way, she had. Despite the fact that he was delighted to have had Tess unwittingly back him up, he found himself wanting to do whatever he could to make Jenny feel better.

Ridiculous. Hell, he'd made her—and himself—nothing but miserable for the last few days. So why was it that *now* he wanted to change all that? And why did he feel so damned lousy?

He inhaled sharply and told himself to get a grip. He wouldn't be doing either of them any favors if he changed his stripes now. Instead, maybe he should just speak up and finish this. While Tess's words were still fresh in her ears, maybe it was time to convince his wife to recognize another truth, too.

For both their sakes.

As Tess turned away, Nick looked at Jenny and said softly, "See? I told you. There is no curse. There is no magic. And there certainly is no Blake Family Lightning Bolt."

Tess screeched to a halt and spun around.

"Oh," she said. "The curse *is* nonsense, I grant you. But the lightning bolt is real."

"What?" Vaguely, Nick was aware of Jenny's triumphant grin. But his gaze was locked on Tess.

She nodded at Nick. "Oh, sure. Felt it myself. The first time my second husband, Clive, kissed me.

Knocked my shoes right off my feet." Tess smiled wistfully at the memory.

For the life of him, he couldn't think of a thing to say.

"And the lightning means you've found your true love, doesn't it?" Jenny asked.

Nick held his breath, waiting. Though he knew the answer even before Tess started talking again.

"Oh, my, yes. Why I would have stayed with Clive forever if it hadn't been for that unfortunate accident with the balloon."

"Balloon?" Nick repeated, despite his best intentions.

"Hot air," Tess told him. "Developed a nasty leak. Of course things might have been different if he hadn't been hovering over a forest at the time."

"Of course." Nick shook his head. Numbly, he watched Jenny leap up from her chair to hug her grandmother.

"Thank you, Tess."

"You're welcome," she said, and gave Jenny a quick kiss. "From the look on your faces, I'm guessing that the Blake Bolt has made an appearance?"

Jenny nodded.

Nick continued to mutter to himself.

"That's lovely," Tess said. "Just remember. The magic isn't in the lightning itself. The magic is in recognizing what you've got when you find it."

Nick glanced up into a pair of wise blue eyes. Instinctively, he knew that when Jenny reached her grandmother's age, her eyes, too, would be filled with the same warmth and wisdom. Irrationally, he found himself wishing that he could be there to see it.

"The lightning just helps you find each other." Tess's gaze shifted from one to the other of them. "The *love* you have to make yourselves."

Nick glanced at Jenny and caught her staring at him. Then she looked down and he followed her gaze to the cheap wedding band he had yet to replace. She ran the tip of one finger over the gold-tone ring and Nick winced as a chip of "gold" flaked off.

He'd meant to buy her another ring. He'd simply forgotten.

Or, his brain whispered, *had you figured that once you bought a* real *ring, the marriage would be real to* you *as well?*

That idea didn't sit well.

"Oh!" Tess interrupted his thoughts and Nick was grateful. "There's one more thing about this true love business."

"Yeah?" he asked hesitantly.

"Stay away from hot air balloons."

In a swirl of black silk, Grandma Tess hurried off to the kitchen, leaving Nick and Jenny to stare at each other across a wall of silence.

Jenny walked into the cozy comfort of the house and paused just over the threshold. She'd had plenty of time to think about everything Tess had said. Nick had hardly spoken during the last couple of hours and after dropping off Tess at her hotel, they'd driven the few miles home in complete quiet.

Tess was right. Not about the curse, of course. Jenny still firmly believed that her grandmother's well-being depended on Jenny and Nick remaining married for the full year. And even if she *hadn't* believed, she wouldn't have been willing to take the risk.

But everything Tess had had to say about the lightning bolt and love was absolutely right. The lightning didn't guarantee true love. How could it? Even magic, she supposed, would be helpless against a man who was dead set on ignoring its existence.

No, feeling the lightning and believing in it were two very different things. And apparently, Nick wasn't ready yet to believe.

So, instead of trying to force Nick into falling in love with her, she would set out to prove that he didn't need to feel responsible for her. She would show him that she was a strong, independent woman capable of taking care of herself. When he was convinced of that, maybe then he'd allow himself to acknowledge the love Jenny was sure he felt for her.

And if he was still unconvinced...well, she would think of something else, that's all.

The door closed softly behind her and Nick tossed his keys onto the nearby table.

"Quite a night," he said softly.

"Yes." *Quite* a night. Between listening to Tess,

watching Nick's reactions and talking to Mama Tarantelli about a job, Jenny was exhausted.

A brief smile flashed across her features as she remembered Mama's pleased response to her request.

"What a good idea," the older woman had cried. "Always, I try to get one of my kids interested in the restaurant. But, no, they all go off to do something else."

"I've never been a waitress, Mama," Jenny had confessed. "But I promise I'll work hard at it."

"Sure, sure you will. Pretty girl like you? Smart, too. You'll be fine." Mama patted Jenny's cheeks with both hands. "You want to start tomorrow, maybe?"

"Tomorrow would be wonderful."

"Good, good. Now go on out there and talk to your grandma while I take care of the sauce."

Jenny had slipped back into the crowded main room of the restaurant without anyone noticing she'd been gone.

A new job. A new town. A new husband.

How quickly her quiet little life had changed. And how wonderful it all could have been, if only Nick would open his eyes and see what they could have together.

"I like your grandmother."

"She likes you, too." Jenny kicked off her heels, bent to pick them up, then started walking toward the bedroom. "I'll miss her."

"She'll be here for a while, won't she?"

"Probably not." Stifling a yawn, she talked around the hand clamped to her mouth. "She said something about hurrying to Egypt. The camel races."

"Camel races?"

"Uh-huh. Tess goes every year."

"Naturally."

Jenny wandered into the bedroom, tossed her high heels onto the floor beside the bed, then snatched up her blue silk robe from the back of a chair.

"Look, Jenny—"

"Nick, I—" she cut him off unintentionally when she spoke at the same time he did. But maybe it was just as well, she told herself. She was simply too tired right then to talk, or argue, or discuss whatever it was he wanted said.

"I'm tired," she told him softly. "I'm just going to go to bed, all right?"

He jerked her a stiff nod and shoved both hands into his pockets. "I guess it'll wait till morning."

Jenny shook her head slightly. "It will have to wait until tomorrow night," she told him. "In the morning, I have to be at work." Then she turned, walked into the bathroom and closed the door behind her.

Work?

Nick stared at the door as if waiting for it to speak and answer all his questions. Yanking his hands out of his pockets, he shoved his fingers through his hair. When did she get a job? And where? Doing what? Jenny? In Vegas? Nick shuddered. The possibilities were too numerous and too frightening to contemplate.

Before he had time to think about what he was doing, he was charging across the floor. He grabbed the doorknob, gave it a turn, threw the door open and stopped dead.

Jenny was just stepping into the shower. Surprised, she whirled around to face him.

Already, steam had filled the tiny room and her hair lay in damp tendrils around her face. Her lips parted slightly, Jenny paused, one foot inside the shower stall, and watched him.

His gaze swept over her naked body and an overpowering ache settled in his groin. Everything he'd wanted to ask her, say to her, vanished from his mind. All he could think of was how long it had been since he'd held her. And how much he'd missed the sensation of losing himself inside her.

Now, no matter what the next day or the next week might bring, he knew that if he couldn't be with her now—tonight—it would kill him. If only briefly, he needed to feel her hands on him. He needed to taste her warmth and know that she loved him.

He took a step toward her and shut the bathroom door, trapping the heat and the steam inside the room with them. He didn't speak. He didn't trust his voice to work around the knot in his throat. But he watched her eyes, her so expressive eyes, carefully. If she made the slightest hint that she wanted him to leave, he would. And he would try to die quietly in a corner somewhere.

Quickly, he yanked his shirt off and absently heard the flying buttons as they landed in different parts of the room. When he tossed the shirt down in a heap, he paused, breath held and waited for a sign from her.

She dipped her head slightly and stepped into the shower. Turning her back to the pulsing shower head, she faced him, water cascading down her shoulders and over her breasts.

He groaned.

She lifted one hand and stretched it out to him in invitation.

In seconds, he undressed and wordlessly joined her under the water, shutting the glass door. So tiny, he thought when she stepped in close to him and wrapped her arms around his waist. Her head barely reached the middle of his chest.

Then her mouth closed over his flat nipple and his brain shut down. Her tongue flicked at his skin as she urged him forward until the water pounded down over them both. Her fingers curled into his waist and he felt the bite of her nails against his back.

He let his hands slide down her spine to caress her wet bottom and he smiled to himself when she moved in his grasp. Her teeth skimmed over his nipple and he tightened his grip on her behind in response. His fingers kneaded her soft, firm flesh and soon she was moaning softly against his chest.

She moved her right hand down, sliding over his

wet body, letting her fingertips arouse him and en-
flame the already blazing fire within him. Then her
small hand slipped between their bodies and her fingers curled around his rock-hard erection.

A guttural groan shot from his throat and his head
fell back on his neck. Her fingers smoothed over him,
teased him and brought him to the edge of madness.
When she reached behind her for a bar of soap, he
was gasping for air, sure he was going to die from
the sheer pleasure she gave him and not minding in
the least.

Slowly, tantalizingly, she rubbed the soap over his
shoulders, his arms, his chest. Her left hand began to
stroke the newly soaped flesh, building a lather that
no water would be able to wash away. Then she
scooped some of the soap bubbles from his chest and
touched them to her own breasts.

"Oh, Jenny, what you do to me," he breathed
heavily, and tried to claim her mouth.

She ducked her head and moved in close to him.
Before he could draw another easy breath, she began
to rub her soapy breasts against his flesh and the slick
glide of skin over skin was almost more than he could
bear.

"You feel so good," she told him, and trailed her
fingertips along the narrow line of dark hair stretched
across his flat belly. When she again found the hard
length of him with her hands, she moaned gently and
confessed, "I've missed you, Nick. I've missed the
feel of you deep inside me." Tilting her head back,

she stared up at him and he felt himself falling into the clear blue pools of her eyes. "I want you so deeply imbedded in me that nothing can tear us apart."

He bent his head and covered her mouth with his own. Parting her lips, his tongue darted in and out of her mouth in a silent promise of things to come. Her breath puffed against his cheek, the shower massage pummeled them both with rhythmic blasts of heat and her fingers continued their gentle assault.

Abruptly, he broke the kiss, reached up behind her and grasped the handle of the shower head. Snapping it from its cradle, he allowed it to hang free for a moment on its long, flexible hose. Hot water rushed at their legs and Jenny's eyes were full of questions. But he wasn't ready to give her any answers yet. For now, he wanted to return some of the torture she'd been dishing out.

Turning her until her back was plastered to his front, Nick nudged her thighs apart with his knee. She sighed and twisted her bottom against his groin and his control threatened to snap. With one arm clamped firmly around her waist, though, he held her still while his other hand reached for the dangling shower head.

"Nick?" she whispered, and tried to move against him again. "What are you doing?"

"Just relax, Jenny," he said softly, nibbling at her ear until she moaned gently. "Relax and feel."

Then he turned the shower head toward her and aimed the pulsating water at her center.

She jerked in his arms, but he held her steady. As the measured, regular pulses of water throbbed at her sex, she began to sway and twist in his grasp. Every time she moved against him, he gritted his teeth tighter, praying for control.

Her breath came in ragged gasps. Her knees trembled and if Nick hadn't been holding her, she would have sagged to the tiled floor. A tormented whimper crawled from her throat and she reached back to wrap both hands around his neck. Her hips began to rock as she sought the unceasing torrents of heat.

He bent his head to kiss her neck and tasted the soapy clean scent of her. He watched as her breasts rose and fell rapidly as a shuddering climax drew near. And just when he thought the trembling would start, she let go of him and pushed the shower head away from her. Spinning around to face him, she went up on her toes and kissed him hard before saying, "No, Nick. I want you. I want it to happen while I hold you inside me."

Something in his chest shattered and splintered into thousands of pieces. Hungrily, he grabbed her and pulled her to him, letting the shower head dangle and bang against the glass doors. He lifted her easily, braced his feet and leaned forward until her back was pressed to the wall.

"Wrap your legs around my waist," he muttered thickly, but she'd already done that.

His body probed at her passage and every touch

was almost unbearable. Release screamed at him. Her moans and throaty whispers begged him not to wait.

Burying his face in the curve of her neck, Nick lowered her onto his shaft. When he was in so deeply he couldn't tell where his body ended and hers began, he started to move.

Her fingers threaded through his hair. Her heels dug into the small of his back. Her damp heat squeezed him tightly, urging him on.

With the hot water pounding at his legs, he thrust himself again and again into her silkiness. When she shouted his name and clutched at him, he felt the tremors ripple through her. And a heartbeat later, he poured everything he was into her warmth.

Twelve

Jenny folded up the sheet neatly, then stacked it on top of the blanket and pillow. Lifting all three, she carried them into the bedroom and set them down on the chair in the corner.

Nick stepped out of the bathroom just as she straightened. Scowling at her, he said for what must have been the thousandth time in the last three days, "Why the hell you have to sleep on the couch is beyond me."

She turned so he wouldn't see the pleased smile that briefly curved her mouth. Since right after their lovemaking session in the shower, she had been spending the nights alone. Oh, she didn't regret what had passed between them. How could she? She loved the fool.

But she wouldn't be able to keep her distance from him by sleeping next to him in a too tempting bed. He might have all the self-control in the world, but she wasn't sure she could keep from cuddling up to him in her sleep. And if she wanted him to figure out on his own that he loved her, then she was going to have to give him the space in which to do it.

Now, only three days into her plan, she thought things were going quite well indeed. Nick was grumpy, cranky, irritable—all of the little things that let her know he was miserable.

"I've already told you," she said as she dragged a brush through her hair quickly. "I think you were right all along. This is simply a marriage of convenience, Nick. There's no reason for us to share a bed."

"What about the curse?" he asked, and leaned against the doorjamb, hands in pockets. "Didn't you say it had to be a *real* marriage?"

"I think it's enough that we're sharing the same house, don't you?"

He grumbled something unintelligible and she hid another smile. Setting the brush on the dresser, she snatched up her purse and walked over to him. She went up on her toes and planted a quick kiss on the corner of his mouth. "It's very sweet of you to be concerned for my grandmother."

"Well, that *is* why we got married..."

"I know." Jenny turned and headed back toward the living room. Now he had to realize that they were meant to *stay* married. "Have a good day," she called over her shoulder.

"Are you going to be home for dinner?"

"I don't think so," she said, without turning to look at him. She'd hardly been in the little house at all the last three days. And she knew her absence was beginning to weigh on him. Whether he knew it or not. "Mama said something about needing extra help tonight."

"That's what she said *last* night."

Jenny stopped walking and half turned toward him. "Nick, it's my job."

He pushed one hand through his hair and walked to stand beside her. "Yeah, I know. But you're never here anymore."

"But, Nick, you're gone all day anyway." Her eyes wide, she stared up at him with what she hoped was an innocently blank expression.

"Yeah, but..."

A horn blasted its way into the conversation and Jenny hurried toward the front door.

"Have to run," she said as she threw the door open and sprinted outside. "My cab's here."

"That's another thing." He followed her down the steps. "You shouldn't be calling cabs. I can take you to the restaurant and pick you up."

Jenny lifted one hand in a wave and kept walking. "That's not necessary. I can manage. Besides, I'm thinking about buying my own car."

She reached the battered yellow taxi, yanked open

the door and climbed inside. As the cab took off like
a launched rocket, she looked back to see Nick, still
standing in the front yard, staring after her.

Nick slid into his usual booth at the rear of Tarantelli's Terrace. His gaze roamed over the roomful
of hungry customers and harried waitresses until he
found his wife.

Balancing a heavy tray that looked nearly as big as
she was, Jenny threaded her way through the crowd
to one of the tables. As she set the legs of a collaps-
ible table and rested the tray atop it, she turned to her
customers and gave them a grin that Nick hadn't seen
directed at him in far too long.

The small cluster of businessmen laughed and
joked with Jenny as she distributed their orders
around the table. When she was finished, she stopped,
pulled her order pad out of her pocket and began to
check it. A bald man to Jenny's right lifted one hand
as if to give her behind a friendly pat.

Nick tensed and came halfway off his seat before
Jenny jumped back out of reach, frowned and wagged
one finger at the man until he ducked his head and
nodded.

Damn it, he told himself. See what could happen?
No matter that Jenny took care of it herself. No matter
that this was his mother's restaurant, not a casino, for
God's sake. No matter even that the would-be groper
was old enough to be Jenny's father. Or that she had
handled him as she would a misbehaving child. It

infuriated Nick to have to sit by and watch his wife dodge roaming hands.

At that instant, his brain reminded him that he didn't have to be there. He *could* be out chasing down bad guys. But the bounty hunter business just didn't seem to interest him much these days. Then, of course, he told himself, he could actually *open* one of the letters his broker had been showering him with recently. Yet, somehow juggling the stock market seemed pretty boring in comparison with Jenny, too.

Hell, he didn't know *what* was wrong with him. Well, except for the obvious fact that he could hardly walk without being in pain. He'd never wanted a woman in his life the way he wanted her. The want didn't ease with the passing of days. It sharpened.

But it wasn't just the lovemaking he missed, he admitted silently. It was Jenny herself. She was hardly at the house anymore. It was almost like it had been before he'd married her. Except that now, when it was just him wandering through the rooms, the little house seemed...emptier. Lonely. And on the rare occasions when she was home, she was too tired to talk to him.

Hell, he wasn't even getting any sleep lately. With her on the couch, he'd discovered that he couldn't sleep without her cuddling up next to him. He found himself lying in the dark, listening for the sounds of her breathing, waiting for her to fling one arm across his chest or to talk in her sleep.

Nick slumped back against the maroon leather-

tufted booth and scowled at the woman who was—
and wasn't—his wife.

When had it happened? When had she become so
important to him?

And what in the hell was he going to do about it?

"Hi, Nick."

He swiveled his head to look at the young waitress
standing beside his table. "Hi, Maegan."

"Back again, huh?" Her short, curly black hair
danced around her cheekbones and her dark green
eyes were flashing with suppressed humor. "Boy,
since Jenny started working here, we're sure seeing a
lot of you."

He ignored the teasing and asked, "How's she doing, anyway?"

"Great." Maegan lifted one shoulder in a half
shrug. "Oh, she dropped a couple of trays and spilled
some drinks on a couple of guys who'd already had
plenty...but otherwise, she's terrific. A born waitress."

"Uh-huh." He wasn't really listening. Instead, his
gaze followed Jenny around the room. Smiling and
laughing with the customers, she *did* seem to enjoy
the work.

"So. You want the usual?"

"Yeah, Maegan," he said. "That'll be fine."

She grinned. "Be right back."

Jenny looked up and met his gaze just then. Nick
smiled and nodded. She lifted one hand and waggled

her fingers at him. Then she was back to work, husband forgotten.

Grumbling under his breath, Nick wished Maegan would hurry up with his beer.

A moment later, a frosty brown bottle slammed down onto the table in front of him. Nick looked up to thank Maegan and instead found himself staring into his mother's sharp, brown eyes.

"So how come you're takin' up one of my tables again, huh?"

"Good to see you, too, Ma."

Mama slid into the booth beside her oldest son and sighed gratefully. "Busy morning."

"Uh-huh."

"Not for you though, huh?"

"What?" Nick tore his gaze from Jenny and looked at his mother.

"I said, you're not so busy. Every day coming down here to sit and stare at your wife."

He shifted uncomfortably and reached for his beer. Lifting it, he took a long drink, then set it back down again. "I'm taking a lunch break."

Mama snorted. "Nice job you got, Nicky. Three-hour lunch breaks."

"Leave it alone, Ma."

"Oh, sure, leave it alone, he says." Mama shook her head and gave Nick's upper arm a quick slap. "You want me to leave it alone, don't bring it to the restaurant."

This wasn't going well, he told himself. But to be

fair, a man needed a good night's sleep if he was going to do battle with Mama. Nick was sorely out of shape.

"That stock man of yours?"

"What?"

"Your man who does all your stocks?"

Jim Torrance. "What about him?"

"Nothin'." Mama shrugged expressively. "Just he called here lookin' for you. Says you don't call him. Don't answer your mail."

"I'll take care of it." Nick sighed and began to scratch at the label on his beer bottle with his thumbnail.

Mama nodded thoughtfully, then took a long, concerned look at her son. "You look tired, Nicky."

"Yeah? That's 'cause I am."

"Oh, you newlyweds." She laughed shortly and shook her head in fond memory. "These are good times for you, Nicky. You should enjoy them."

Oh, right. Life was just a barrel of laughs right now.

"That Jenny's a good girl," Mama said softly. "I like her."

"I'm glad."

"She's not like the other one."

"Ma, I don't want to talk about it."

"Too bad. I'm the mother here. *I* make the rules."

Damn it. He sure as hell wasn't in the mood to discuss Angela and Tony.

"A long time now, Nicky," Mama said slowly, "I

think you've been blaming yourself for Tony being gone."

It seemed that he didn't have a choice.

"Ma…"

"Shut up now, it's my turn." She smiled to take the sting out of the reprimand, but went right on talking. "Angela took Tony and Tony went. You didn't have anything to do with it."

"If I hadn't married her in the first place, Tony would never have met her."

"Oh, well, sure." Mama slapped the tabletop. "And if I hadn't gone to the Sons of Italy dance one fine Saturday night, I never would have met your papa and you wouldn't have been born to marry Angela." She reached up and grabbed Nick's chin with her fingertips. Giving his head a little shake, she asked, "So. Does that make it *my* fault Tony left with that…woman?"

"Of course not."

"And it's not yours, either." Clucking her tongue at him, she leaned forward and kissed him, at the same time giving his other cheek a swift, soft slap. "Stop this now, Nicky. Before you let that woman steal *two* of my sons."

He stared into those chocolate brown eyes and found the love he'd always counted on waiting for him. Chuckling to himself, Nick acknowledged that he also saw impatience and frustration in his mother's eyes.

Hell, maybe she was right. Maybe it was finally

time to put the past behind him—before it gobbled up his future. A future he might be able to build with Jenny. If he could bring himself to risk another failure.

"All right, Ma," he said, draping one arm around her shoulders and pulling her close. "I'll think about it."

"Good. At least you got smart in time to see how lucky you are with Jenny."

He wasn't so sure about that. Oh, he knew he was lucky to have found her. He just didn't know if luck was enough.

"You know, Nicky..."

"What?"

"Jenny was feeling bad when she got to work this morning." Mama glanced at the ceiling. "Maybe we've got a baby coming?"

A *baby?*

He darted a look at his mother, then his gaze shot across the crowded restaurant to Jenny. She didn't look any different, he thought, then immediately laughed at himself. How different should she be? If she was pregnant, the baby couldn't be more than a few weeks along.

Quickly, his mind raced back. To the honeymoon. Those three incredible days in the plush suite. From there, his thoughts leapt to a few nights ago and their interlude in the shower. His groin tightened and he just managed to muffle a groan.

Okay, sure. A baby was possible. Like some teenage idiot, he hadn't taken any precautions at all. He could blame his stupidity on the honeymoon on a misunderstanding. But that night in the shower? That time was his own damn fault. He'd known she wasn't protected and it hadn't stopped him for a minute. Frowning slightly, he wondered if maybe his subconscious had been at work. Maybe there was a small part of him that *hoped* she would get pregnant.

Nick rubbed one hand across his jaw and tried to ignore the leap of emotion inside him. Instead he told himself that the odds of a surprise pregnancy were pretty slim.

Besides, if Jenny was pregnant, she'd have said so. She was too honest to keep a thing like that from him. A hollow, empty feeling settled in his stomach and Nick realized with a start that he was almost disappointed. "Not much chance of that, Ma."

She snorted and waved one hand at him. "Dino told me. He says you never left your room at the hotel. So what were you two doing for three days? Checkers, maybe?" Her features softened slightly. "Your papa, God rest him, gave me four babies, no trouble at all."

Hmm. Nick frowned thoughtfully. Three long days. Two even longer nights. The shower. Maybe there was more of a chance than he'd thought.

A baby.

The idea was both exciting and terrifying.

He looked for Jenny and when he located her, his

imagination took over. In his mind's eye, he saw her small form big and round with his child. Their child.

His mouth went dry and something warm and precious roared up inside him. Nick imagined her holding their baby, cooing at it. Kissing it good-night and then turning to him. His imagination conjured up the image of Jenny and him, staring down at their sleeping child, wrapped in a warm glow of something he'd never expected to find.

Love.

How could he have been so stupid?

"See ya later, Ma."

"Sure, sure," she mumbled as he slid out of the booth and began to work his way toward Jenny.

As he got close, he saw her stumble slightly on a patch of spilled water and Nick's heart staggered, too. He hurried his steps and when he got close enough, he grabbed her upper arm in a firm, gentle grip.

"Nick?" She looked up at him. "What are you doing?"

"Whoa, Jenny." He swore as he glanced down at the high heels she was wearing. "You shouldn't be wearing those now."

"Oh," she shrugged. "Don't worry, they're comfortable."

"But if you fell," he persisted, "you could hurt the baby."

"What baby?"

"It's all right..." he said with a smile, and pulled her in close to him. "Mama told me."

Jenny pushed away from his chest and looked across the room until she spotted her mother-in-law. Mama, far from being contrite, lifted both hands in an eloquent shrug and grinned from ear to ear.

"Good Lord," Jenny muttered, and grabbed Nick's hand. She didn't know whether to laugh or be furious with her interfering mother-in-law. Certainly Mama had meant well. But what good would it do if Nick only wanted her because he thought she was pregnant? Dragging him along behind her, she marched through the kitchen and out the back door.

Hot, desert air slapped at her, stealing her breath away. A gusty wind roared through the parking lot, carrying the scent of coming rain.

Jenny pushed her windblown hair out of her eyes and glared at her husband. "I'm not pregnant!"

His smile faded just a bit. "But Mama said—"

"Mama is wrong."

"Are you sure?"

"As sure as I can be," she snapped. Her cycle had kicked in right on time, assuring her that there would be no baby from their nights in the Taj.

"Oh." He frowned, then brightened again. "But what about the other night in the shower? We didn't use anything then, either."

True. She couldn't be completely positive there was no child until her cycle struck again. This wouldn't even be happening, she told herself, if she'd only had the kind of social life that required her to take the Pill.

A baby?

A husband and child. All the family she'd ever dreamed of.

How excited she would have been. If everything between them were settled. She stared up at her husband and watched him squint against the wind and sun. Jenny loved him. But she wouldn't be staying with him—or taking another risk on creating a new life with him—until he could admit to the feelings he had for her.

And now, she thought, was as good a time as any to force his hand. She might have been willing to let him come to his own conclusions in his own good time—if there wasn't a possible child to consider.

Taking a step toward him, she met his gaze squarely and said, "But if I was pregnant, it wouldn't be any of your business."

"What?"

She ignored his incredulous expression.

"You've made it clear that you want this marriage to be just what it started out to be, Nick. Temporary."

"We're not talking about us, Jenny." He raked his hand through his hair to keep it out of his eyes. "We're talking about our baby."

"And what if there is no baby?" She shook her head slowly and shouted over the rising wind. "What then?"

"Jenny, I—"

"I know—Angela and Tony," she broke in sharply.

"They have nothing to do with us."

"They have *everything* to do with us."

Nick turned, stomped off in the opposite direction and came right back after taking only a few steps.

"Don't you understand?" he said, bending to look her directly in the eye. "Because of me, my brother's been gone five years."

She shook her head. "Tony left because he wanted to. Angela left because *she* wanted to." Nick's features tightened stubbornly, but Jenny plowed right ahead. "As much as you want to take responsibility for everything that happens in the world, you can't. They made their decisions. They're *happy*. Your mother, Dino, Gina—none of them blame you. You're the only one insisting on punishing yourself."

He straightened, faced into the wind and frowned.

Jenny laid her left hand on his arm and waited until he looked down at her. "I was hoping that you would come to see how good we are together. But if you're willing to let me walk out of your life just to pay some imaginary debt, then you don't deserve me."

He winced and covered her hand with one of his own. His thumb smoothed over the flaked, cheap wedding ring on her finger. "Almost every guy I know has made a mess out of his marriage." Nick's gaze lifted to meet hers. "I don't want to fail again."

"Well, then," she said softly, and he bent closer to hear her over the wind. "Maybe it's time you stopped acting like a *guy* and started acting like a man." A flash of pain shot through his eyes and she almost regretted what she'd said.

Almost.

At least, she told herself, whatever happened now, she'd had her say and done her best to reach him. The rest was up to Nick. Slowly she pulled her hand out from under his and went back to work.

An hour later the last of the lunch hour crowd still mobbed the restaurant. Rain pounded on the roof, slashed at the windows and the accompanying wind howled through the trees surrounding the building.

Jenny smiled absently, handed a customer his check and turned back toward her station. Lifting her chin, she blinked away a sheen of tears and finally admitted to herself that Nick wasn't going to come rushing in out of the parking lot to declare his undying love.

Undoubtedly he'd left when the storm hit and, right now, he was probably sitting comfortably in his little house, enjoying the quiet and planning for the day that she would move out.

"Why don't you take a break?"

"Hmm?" She looked up into Maegan's concerned features and shook her head. "No, thanks. I'd rather keep busy." That way she wouldn't have to remember all the hideous things she'd said to Nick that had driven him off.

"Jenny!"

The shout was loud enough to be heard over the rain, the wind and the clatter of dishes.

She stepped out of the waitress's station and looked at the front door.

Nick stood just inside the restaurant. His wet hair was plastered to his skull, his clothes looked as though someone had shoved him into a pool and his eyes were wild as they scanned the startled faces turned toward him.

He looked wonderful.

Then he spotted Jenny and his features softened, brightened. Wiping his face free of rainwater with one hand, he started across the room, bumping into chairs and jostling tables. He kept up a steady string of "Excuse me's, pardon me's," but never took his eyes off her. It was as though she was all he could see.

When he finally reached her side, he grabbed her, pulled her close and claimed her mouth in a kiss that left her breathless.

Cold and damp soaked into her from Nick's clothing, but she felt indescribably warm. Hope shimmered to life inside her and the heat it brought warmed all the corners of her soul. As he broke the kiss and lifted his head to look at her, she prayed she wasn't reading too much into his actions.

Someone behind her started clapping their hands and Jenny had a sneaking suspicion it was Mama. But she was too entranced with the expression in her husband's eyes to care.

Their gazes locked, Nick dropped to one knee in

front of her. Taking her left hand in his, he slowly pulled the tawdry wedding band off. She held her breath, and realized just how naked her finger felt without that ring. In seconds though, he reached into his pocket, then tenderly replaced her wedding ring with a new one. She stared down at the wide gold band crowned with a star sapphire surrounded by diamonds.

Her jaw dropped.

"It's the color of your eyes," he said softly.

A shaky breath rushed from her and her vision was blurred by tears she didn't bother to hide this time.

Vaguely, Nick heard a hush settle over the interested crowd behind him. Absently, he noted his mother in the background, fairly jumping up and down in delight. But none of them meant anything to him. All he could see, all he ever wanted to see, was the love shining in Jenny's blue eyes.

In a loud, clear voice, he asked, "Jenny Tarantelli, will you marry me again?"

She bit down on her bottom lip and he watched tears spill over her eyes and roll down her cheeks. Silently he promised himself that he would spend the rest of his life making sure she never had a reason to cry again. If she gave him that chance.

Seconds ticked by and she still hadn't answered him. Beginning to worry a bit, he cradled her left hand in both of his and said, more softly this time, "Please marry me, Jenny. For real. Forever." Still no answer. She only cried and stared at him as if seeing him for the first time.

Slowly he stood, cupped her face in his hands and bent to press a short, sweet kiss to her lips. "I love you, Jenny. Be my wife."

She took one long, shuddering breath, then reached up and brushed his wet hair off his forehead. "I love you, too. And forever isn't nearly long enough."

His heart started beating again.

With the applause of the crowd ringing in their ears, he scooped her up into his arms and headed for the front door.

Several hours later Jenny stretched lazily then ran one hand down her husband's naked body. He groaned quietly.

"You're killing me, Jenny."

She'd never felt better. And though her husband claimed to be exhausted and spent, she wasn't quite finished with him yet. Her fingers teased him into arousal again and as he pulled her on top of him, she laughed. "For a dying man, you seem to be in surprisingly good form."

His hands slid down her spine to cup her bottom and she stopped laughing. Tendrils of expectation skittered through her bloodstream and the Blake Family Lightning Bolt shimmered in the air between them. Slowly she pushed herself into a sitting position and straddled him. Raising up on her knees, she teased him with her nearness. "Mama's expecting grandbabies soon. You don't want to disappoint her, do you?''

Nick grinned, grabbed her hips and slowly lowered her onto his hardened flesh. She groaned and let her head fall back as he filled her.

When they were joined again, as they were meant to be, he whispered. ''We don't dare disappoint Mama.''

Jenny moved against him, then leaned down to kiss him gently.

Nick groaned and muttered, ''If we keep this up, though, we're going to need a much bigger house....''

* * * * *

As seen on TV!
Free Gift Offer

With a Free Gift proof-of-purchase from any Silhouette® book,
you can receive a beautiful cubic zirconia pendant.

This gorgeous marquise-shaped stone is a genuine cubic
zirconia—accented by an 18" gold tone necklace.

(Approximate retail value $19.95)

Send for yours today...
compliments of ♥ *Silhouette*®

To receive your free gift, a cubic zirconia pendant, send us one original proof-of-
purchase, photocopies not accepted, from the back of any Silhouette Romance™,
Silhouette Desire®, Silhouette Special Edition®, Silhouette Intimate Moments®
or Silhouette Yours Truly™ title available in February, March and April at your favorite
retail outlet, together with the Free Gift Certificate, plus a check or money order for
$1.65 U.S./$2.15 CAN. (do not send cash) to cover postage and handling, payable
to Silhouette Free Gift Offer. We will send you the specified gift. Allow 6 to 8 weeks for
delivery. Offer good until April 30, 1997 or while quantities last. Offer valid in the
U.S. and Canada only.

Free Gift Certificate

Name: _____

Address: _____

City: _____ State/Province: _____ Zip/Postal Code: _____

Mail this certificate, one proof-of-purchase and a check or money order for postage
and handling to: SILHOUETTE FREE GIFT OFFER 1997. In the U.S.: 3010 Walden
Avenue, P.O. Box 9077, Buffalo NY 14269-9077. In Canada: P.O. Box 613, Fort Erie,
Ontario L2Z 5X3.

FREE GIFT OFFER   084-KFD
ONE PROOF-OF-PURCHASE
To collect your fabulous FREE GIFT, a cubic zirconia pendant, you must include this
original proof-of-purchase for each gift with the properly completed Free Gift Certificate.
